# BOOK 1 BLOOD DRAGON

## THE DRAGON PRINCE OF IJLAL

# MICAH JOHNSON

GLASSSPIDERPUBLISHING

Cover design by Judith S. Design & Creativity
www.judithsdesign.com
Published by Glass Spider Publishing
www.glassspiderpublishing.com

*When I started this project, I never imagined I would also end up battling cancer at the same time. To all of my doctors and nurses, especially the ones who thought I was a teacher as I edited furiously while they were pumping me full of life-saving poison. To my editor, who has the patience of a saint. To my mom, who has never been anything but supportive, and my dad who will do anything to help me realize a dream. To my friends and family, who all encouraged me in your own little ways. To my third-grade teacher, Dawna Underwood, who saw and encouraged my love for stories even after I left your class. And to Wendy Alford, who I have known at least that long, and without whom I probably never would have started actually writing my stories down. To every person I met along the way, this story is for you.*

# CHAPTER 1



*Why is your answer always more death?*

Seiko lay on his mat in the corner of the room he shared with his brother, back pressed against the wall. It was his least favorite day of the entire year: the day his father, the Dragon King of Ijlal, received his yearly tribute from his subjects.

All around the world, there were dragons, and then there were blood dragons. Blood dragons fed off fear, pain, and despair. Unlike regular dragons, they didn't hoard jewels or gold but instead traveled the world killing and terrorizing people and animals wherever they found them.

Ijlal's rulers were regular, shape-shifting dragons. They sought out bounties of gold and precious gems with an insatiable appetite. Dragons like Seiko and his family had been created in the void between the stars by celestial forces and cast down onto the planet in egg-shaped meteors, where they hatched and generally grew up to terrorize the populace.

Most dragons filled caves with jewels and burned farmers' crops to the ground, but Ryu had a different approach. Ijlal was a country rich in gemstones and mineral wealth. Many wars had been fought over mining rights, and she had a history of exploiting her own people. Ryu promised the people protection and safety for a portion of their profits. Exhausted and downtrodden, the people would have agreed to anything.

For the first few years, Ryu was true to his word, and Ijlal knew prosperity and peace the likes of which they'd never dreamed possible. But every year, Ryu's greed grew. He demanded more and more tribute, sucking the land dry of its resources.

Those who couldn't fulfill Ryu's demands were killed for his pleasure. He would transform into a giant orange dragon on a whim and hunt his subjects and their livestock. The way he seemed to feed off their fear and despair, you could almost mistake him for a blood dragon.

The fact his people were suffering was of little consequence to the Dragon King of Ijlal. When his own subjects could no longer fulfill his demands and their fear of him became routine, he turned his attention to the neighboring country of Sedria. This proved to be a mistake, as Sedria's two battle masters, her Wolf and Raven, were the greatest tacticians and warriors on the continent. It was even rumored that the Raven of Sedrian Intelligence was a servant of Death, one of Zagreus' top lieutenants. That war had ended with Ryu retaining control of Ijlal but being forced to pay his own tithe to Sedria, which caused him to put even more pressure on his subjects.

Each household was required to bring a specified amount of gold or precious stones but, largely due to the dragon's ravenous desire for such things, fineries were becoming increasingly rare in Ijlal. There was always some poor farmer or tradesman who couldn't find or afford the required tribute and in desperation tried to substitute it with goods or services. That always ended in bloodshed. The only thing Ryu loved more than accumulating vast amounts of gold and jewels was seeing the abject terror on his subjects' faces whenever he looked at them or growled in their direction.

Seiko sighed and pushed himself to his feet. He wanted to just lie on his mat and skip the whole day. Maybe then he could block out the screams. But he knew his brother would be back soon, and Kana was just as violent as their father.

As if conjured by his thoughts, the door flew open. Seiko threw himself to the side as a dagger sailed through the air and buried itself in his pillow. "I'm up, Kana!" Seiko growled, glaring at him.

Kana was thirteen, four years older than Seiko. He had short-cropped metallic black hair and unsettling yellow eyes. His outfit was all black, and he wore a ridiculously ornate and jewel-encrusted crown on his head. He elbowed Seiko in the ribs as he brushed past him to retrieve his dagger. "Father wants us out in the courtyard in thirty minutes, and you'd better not embarrass him."

"I'll be there. Now leave me alone."

"You sure you don't need help?" Kana asked with a grin as he kicked the ruined pillow, scattering feathers everywhere.

Seiko glared at him, hands balled into fists, but when Kana took a step toward him, he backed away. "Last time you helped me, I was poisoned."

Kana shrugged and headed for the door. "Still can't prove it was me."

Sighing, Seiko closed and locked the door then got ready for the day. When he was finished, he looked himself over in the giant mirror on a stand next to Kana's bed. As much as he hated this entire day, he knew he needed to pass his father's inspection.

Seiko had wiry silver hair and pale blue eyes. His outfit was all gray with tight sleeves and a pair of tight, jewel-encrusted gold bracers attached to his wrists. He shook his head as he straightened his collar, wondering again if the bracers were his father's way of reminding him that he was trapped.

"Better get going," a voice said. "You already know you're not gonna do what he wants. You don't want to be late, too."

Seiko turned around with brows knit, glancing at the still-locked door. "Korbin, the door's locked. How did you even get in here?"

Korbin was the resident troublemaker. As far as Seiko knew, the boy had no family and lived off whatever he could steal. He was seven years old and small for his age. He had fine, shaggy black hair that fell incessantly in front of his face. His eyes were small and dark. He had a beak-like nose and a small mouth with thin lips. His outfit was made of rags and other children's discarded clothing. Korbin never wore shoes, and the only part of his outfit that remained unchanged was the tattered black cape that seemed to drift around him like smoke.

"I had a ghost pull me through the wall," Korbin said, eyes widening.

Seiko rolled his eyes. It said something about the state of his own life that the only person he could call a friend was a bitter, crazy orphan who thrived on chaos. "Why are you here?"

"To make sure you're not late," came the impatient reply as Korbin pushed Seiko toward the door. "Don't want to give Ryu extra reasons to be mad at you."

"I'm going, I'm going," Seiko muttered as he left the castle and strode into the courtyard.

It was large enough to hold maybe five hundred subjects, plus soldiers and livestock, with a wooden platform set against the castle wall. That was where Ryu would receive his tribute. The soldiers at the gate and stationed on the walls monitored everyone entering and exiting, and the line outside stretched for miles.

Seiko took a deep breath, squared his shoulders, straightened his spine, and headed for the platform. He took his place beside

Kana, his right hand clasping his left forearm just below the elbow as trumpets blew and the ceremony began.

*     *     *

It was nearly dusk, and there had been no major incidences of violence. Seiko looked at the dwindling line of supplicants daring to hope they might make it through the whole day without a death. Those hopes were dashed when a man stumbled forward, trembling. Behind him were a pair of surprisingly healthy cows who were not at all thrilled to be this close to a trio of dragons.

Seiko heard the guards snickering. Clearly, the man had been roughed up on his way through the gate.

Beside him, Kana chuckled, and Seiko's hands clenched as Kana said, "This idiot brought cows. Cows! This should be fun."

Seiko looked up at his father, hoping for leniency, but instead saw that Ryu had become dangerously bored with the day's proceedings. He was disinclined to be merciful even in a good mood. He would not be kind.

Standing well over six feet tall, made even taller by the raised platform, Ryu towered over everyone in the courtyard. He had a full beard and thick, wiry, metallic-orange hair. He stepped toward the man, who fell to his knees and began to sob.

"What have you brought me?" Ryu asked, his deep voice booming across the courtyard.

"Sire, I am merely a poor farmer. I… I have no gold or precious jewels, and no one is willing to trade them. I have brought you my most prized possessions: the finest heifers in all the land."

Seiko looked from Ryu to Kana and groaned, seeing nothing but bloodlust in their eyes.

"Tribute is gold, jewels, or a life," Ryu said slowly. "Which category do your bovine fall into?"

"N-none, sire," the man whispered, head bowed.

Ryu's eyes lit up as he drew his dagger. The blade was crafted from obsidian and sharpened to the point that it could easily cut even a dragon's thick hide. He turned and held the dagger out to Seiko, eyes glittering. "Kill him."

Seiko looked down at the poor man who was on his knees pleading for his life, then back up at Ryu and Kana, who were watching him eagerly. He knew exactly how to gain his father's approval. He could take the dagger and open the man's carotid artery with a single flick of his wrist. In less than a second, the damage would be done. The farmer would die a dramatic death, blood spraying everywhere. It would horrify the crowd and delight the dragons. But he couldn't do it. He knew that nothing he did would prevent the man's death, but he couldn't make himself take an innocent life just to satisfy his father. Shaking his head slowly, Seiko backed away from Ryu.

Before the crowd could realize what had happened, Kana stepped forward, took the dagger from his father's outstretched hand, and slashed it across the farmer's throat.

Seiko turned away, stomach roiling at the sight. Ryu grabbed Seiko by the collar and half dragged, half carried him into the palace. Kana followed, grinning, the bloody dagger still clutched in his hand.

Servants threw themselves out of the way of the furious dragon king as Ryu burst into his study and threw Seiko across the room. Seiko groaned as his head bounced off the hardwood bookcase. Groping, he pushed himself to his feet. Kana followed, locking the study's heavy wooden doors behind him.

The room was richly furnished with various ceremonial weapons affixed to the walls and an armchair facing an unlit fireplace.

Covering the rough stone floor was a soft area rug, and a heavy oak desk sat on the other side of the room. The study had two doors: the one through which they'd entered, and the servants' passage. There were no windows and no other means of escape. There were six wall sconces framing the doors and fireplace. They burst alight with an irritated glance from Ryu.

"Why did you refuse to kill him?" Ryu demanded, pacing. "Why do you refuse to become the creature you were meant to be?"

Kana perched on the chair's armrest, watching Seiko with a crazed smile on his lips.

"He didn't deserve death," Seiko said. "His offer of the pair of cows was fair. And honestly, they were worth more than some of the gems you've collected." Although he spoke softly, when he raised his head to look at his father, there was no submission in his eyes.

"I don't want cows!" Ryu yelled. "I want gold!"

"But if you had a decent herd, you wouldn't have to turn into a dragon and hunt your subjects' animals, burning everything in your path," Seiko said earnestly, his hands moving as he talked. "They're starving and afraid enough of us as it is."

Ryu smacked Seiko so hard that he stumbled back a few paces. Kana moved to block Seiko's path to the room's other door, dagger still wet with blood.

"If they did not fear us, they would tear us apart as they did the rest of my kin!" Ryu roared.

"They forced that fight, warring over the precious stones and metals of Ijlal. It's wrong, father. You are wrong. We shouldn't be the monsters that haunt their dreams, and we don't have to be," Seiko said, blinking back tears as a stinging handprint appeared on his cheek.

"Don't pretend like morality matters," Kana sneered. "The

strong enslave the weak, and we are the strong."

Ryu folded his arms across his chest and glared at Seiko. "We are dragons. Monsters. It's past time you learned to accept that and use it to your advantage."

Seiko shook his head as tears rolled down his face. "I just… I can't do what you do, Father. These people…they're innocent. They made you king because you promised to protect them. Instead, you broke them."

Ryu clenched his teeth and grabbed Seiko by the shirtfront, lifting him off his feet. "You will learn to hate if it kills you. You are my son. You will act like it."

"Why is your answer always more death?" Seiko demanded in frustration, eyes flashing. "What did they ever do except cower in fear of you?"

Ryu threw him across the room with a roar. Seiko crashed into the wall and crumpled to the ground with a groan.

Before Ryu could close the distance, Kana darted forward and stabbed Seiko in the arm. Seiko cried out and grabbed the dagger, holding it in place. Ryu grabbed Kana by the arm and jerked him back. "We do not stab each other. I will not have either of you setting fire to the drapes again."

Kana bowed his head. "Yes, Father."

"Roll up that rug and make sure there's nothing else that's combustible near your brother," he ordered.

Kana hurried to obey.

Seiko grimaced. Something strange was happening within the wound. He'd never been stabbed before; Ryu frowned on drawing dragon blood due to its tendency to spontaneously combust, but he hadn't expected it to…burn like this. He knew better than to remove the dagger before his father was ready.

At last, Ryu reached out and jerked the dagger from Seiko's arm.

The boy cried out, pressing a hand against the wound. Ryu stared at the dagger as the blade bubbled and hissed, already half its original size.

Seiko looked down in horror as his silver blood began to eat his shirt.

Ryu dropped the dagger and it struck the floor with a clatter. They watched as the blood dissolved everything around it, including the floor. All three of them were silent as the dagger continued to hiss and curl in on itself and the room filled with the acrid smell of burning metal. Finally, the corrosion subsided. All that was left of the dagger was a deformed, twisted mass of metal resting in an indentation on the floor where the stone itself had been eaten away.

"Tower. Now," Ryu ordered, his voice hoarse.

Seiko looked up at Ryu and Kana, eyes wide. The atmosphere in the room had turned dark the instant the dagger came out of his arm, and he was terrified of what it meant. He skirted around Kana and fled out through the servants' passage. As the door slammed closed behind him, Ryu roared with anger.

Dodging servants and boxes filled with the day's tribute to be sorted and added to Ryu's hoard, Seiko sprinted through the palace and up to the tower. He reached the top of the staircase and pushed the heavy door open, collapsing in the center of the room, gasping for breath. Behind him, the door fell shut under its own weight. He was trapped until and unless someone came for him.

Seiko pushed himself to his knees and removed his ruined shirt, tearing the bracers from his arms. His blood had stopped oozing and had begun to harden over the wound. He quickly changed into the spare set of clothes he kept in the tower and looked around him.

The room was circular with polished stone walls. There was one slit of a window opposite the door. The room was devoid of furnishings except for a candle stub, a tattered old blanket, and a dirty chamber pot. He began to pace, occasionally pulling up his shirtsleeve to look at his wound.

The thought crossed his mind that he should have run when he'd had the chance. "Where would I even go?" he snorted.

It was the question that had always prevented him from running. Even if he could escape the palace, he knew no one in Ijlal would risk Ryu's wrath to aid him—and as a silver-haired dragon, his disguise options were limited. Past that, there was nowhere for him to run. The neighboring country was Sedria, and while they had the army and political clout to protect him, it just wasn't an option. Seiko shuddered at the mere thought. Sedria was home to the only two people in the world Ryu feared: the Ruby Salamander and the Grim Reaper's avatar, Argus the All-Seeing. Surely, they would kill him on sight.

Seiko let out a rush of breath as his legs gave out beneath him. "Father is going to have me killed."

"What makes you say that?" a soft voice asked.

Seiko shot to his feet and looked around the dark room, heart hammering. The only light was a small sliver of moonlight shining through the cell's narrow window. "Who's there?"

"Is that truly what matters at this moment?" the voice responded. It was deep and echoing, as if having traveled down a long, empty tunnel to reach him, yet it felt like the presence was right beside him.

Seiko cocked his head, brows knit. The voice was familiar, but no face came to mind, which was unusual for him.

"Why would he want to kill you?" the voice repeated.

"I don't know!" Seiko said as he began to pace the room. "It was just a normal day. I mean, I did refuse to murder the farmer, but it isn't the first time. Father had to be expecting that."

"Then what changed?"

Seiko stopped pacing and looked down at his wound. "Kana stabbed me," he whispered.

"Ah," the voice said sadly. "Then they have begun to understand."

"Understand what? What do you know? Who are you?" Seiko demanded.

"What matters is getting you to safety," the voice said, ignoring Seiko's questions. "Killing a being like you is an inherently difficult task, but given enough time, Ryu could manage it."

"Why should I listen to you?" Seiko growled. "You won't even tell me who you are."

The voice let out a breathy sigh. "Life is full of decisions you will have to make without sufficient knowledge, my son. In this case, your choice is simple. You either allow me to help you save your own life, or you wait here patiently while Ryu devises the best way to end it. What do you have to lose?"

"Not much, I guess," Seiko muttered. "I'm probably dead either way. How do you plan on getting me out of this tower?"

"Come to the window."

Seiko hesitated but did as he was told.

"Now take out your knife and cut your arm."

"You want me to bleed," Seiko realized. "Why is my blood any different from Kana's?"

"Your blood acts as an acid when it comes into contact with earth matter. You should be able to use it to widen this opening enough to slip through."

"Yeah I picked up on that," Seiko said, pulling out his knife. "But what does that really accomplish? We're at the top of a tower. How does opening a hole in the wall help me escape? I mean, I guess I could try and transform on the way down, but it's not a quick process."

"Trust…" the voice whispered as it faded.

Seiko shrugged and winced as he slid the blade of his knife along the inside of his left forearm, watching as his silver blood bubbled and hissed against the metal. He smeared his blood on the windowsill and watched in horrified fascination as it corroded the stone enough for him to squeeze out. He sat in the opening, willing his blood to stop flowing, and watched in amazement as it hardened and fused with his arm.

"Now what?" he asked as the wind whipped around him.

"Who's there?" a voice called from above him.

Seiko craned his neck and leaned out as far as he could without falling. He recognized the voice, but it wasn't the same as what had been guiding him thus far. He squinted into the darkness. There was a scrabbling sound, and a head popped out over the roof. "Korbin?" he asked in surprise. "It's Seiko. Is there someone up there with you?"

Korbin's head poked over the lip of the roof as he peered down at Seiko. "Nobody up here but me. They'd be too heavy to carry, anyway. But what are you doing, and how did you do that?" he asked, pointing at the hole in the tower wall Seiko was sitting in.

"That's…kind of a long story," Seiko said. "I think Kana and my father want to kill me."

"Oh, they definitely do." Korbin let out a cackle. "They're still arguing over how to do it, though."

"Wonderful," Seiko sighed under his breath. "What are you doing up here, anyway?"

"Messing with the staff, what else?" Korbin held up a sandwich and an emerald ring.

Seiko shook his head. "I don't even want to know where or how you got that ring. But how did you get up to the roof?"

"I flew," Korbin said with a crazy smile.

Seiko ran his tongue over his dry lips and tried again. "How are you going to get down?"

"Oh, I brought a rope." Korbin's head disappeared then reappeared, dropping the end of a long rope down to Seiko. "It doesn't reach all the way to the ground, but it's better than taking a flying leap."

"Do you mind if I use it?" Seiko asked, eyeing the drop.

"Sure, but go fast," Korbin warned. "I'm not supposed to be up here, and the guards like to use me as target practice."

"Of course they do," Seiko said as he grabbed the rope and dropped down the side of the tower using his hands and feet to slow his descent as much as he dared. He fell the last twelve feet, biting his tongue in an attempt to muffle his screams as he landed and felt something in his leg give way.

Korbin was beside him in an instant. It occurred to Seiko that there was no way Korbin could have made it off the roof that fast, but soldiers began shouting as Korbin dragged him to his feet. Seiko limped after Korbin, teeth clenched against the pain. Korbin grabbed Seiko's arm and pulled him in between a row of stalls, using the horses' bodies to hide them as soldiers rushed past.

"How are we supposed to get out?" Seiko asked with a groan.

Korbin watched him, beady eyes boring into him. Seiko shifted uncomfortably. "Hard to believe you're everything he claims, but he doesn't know how to lie," Korbin said. "We're not getting out. The portcullis is open, but one of us has to be a distraction. It has to be me since I'm not injured and I'm not the one they want dead. Once I've distracted the guards, take one of the horses and run."

Seiko grabbed Korbin's wrist. "Look, I don't know why you're helping me, and I'm not stupid enough to believe you don't have an ulterior motive. But let me just say thank you, and good luck."

Korbin laughed. It was a dark sound that set Seiko's teeth on edge. "I make my own luck, and it's rarely ever good," he said and disappeared into the night.

Seiko glanced out of the stables at the gate. The large metal portcullis was open, but he knew it could drop very quickly and that the spiked ends could shear straight through bone. His stomach turned as he went back into the stables and opened a stall door. It was about time for the evening patrol to head out, so that horse was already tacked up and ready. Seiko tried to mount the nervous animal as quietly as possible. Just as he settled himself on the horse's back, there was a maniacal laugh followed by a loud thud and a dozen screams of pain. Seiko let out a cry as the horse bolted. Carrying him along, it flew through the open portcullis.

Hearing fighting up on the walls, Seiko pulled up on the horse's reins and looked back, searching for Korbin in the dark. He heard Korbin's cackle, but the horse screamed and bolted as it was hit by an arrow, tearing the reins from Seiko's hands. He clung to the horse's mane as the wind whipped around them and the screams faded.

Seiko didn't look up until the horse finally plodded to a stop, legs shaking. Three hours had gone by, and Sieko could barely keep his eyes open as he swayed in the saddle, even with the horse stationary. Instead of the mountains surrounding the castle, he found himself in rolling farmland abutting a forest. When he tried to dismount, he was so tired that he mostly just rolled off the horse. He fell with a cry as his legs gave way beneath him.

Gritting his teeth, he forced himself into a sitting position and looked around. He was on what looked like a game trail at the edge of a forest. He removed the boot and sock of his left foot and bit back a scream. His lower leg was swollen and purple. He tried to wiggle his toes and groaned in pain.

"What do I do now?" he exclaimed, wiping his eyes with his sleeve.

"Now it is my turn to help you, Tukiko," a woman said.

Seiko's head snapped up to see a figure standing at the edge of the forest. His eyes narrowed as he studied the woman. She had thick black hair that fell freely down to her waist, and there were flowers and vines woven throughout. She wore a brown dress and a deep-green cloak.

"What did you call me, and who are you?" Seiko demanded, flinching as the woman approached and knelt before him.

"You may call me Aderes," she said, smiling reassuringly.

Before Seiko could react, the woman placed her hands on either side of his injured leg and squeezed. He screamed and tried to kick her with his good leg, but the grass he sat on grew up suddenly around him and held him down.

"I'm sorry about that," Aderes said softly as she rose. Seiko's eyes widened as the grass released him. "We don't have much time. Your brother is on his way, and he is not happy." She knelt before him again, this time carrying a sturdy tree branch. "You broke your leg when you fell from the tower. I need to splint it so it doesn't move."

Seiko stiffened when she touched him again but watched her work with interest. When she was finished, she walked out of his field of vision and returned with a fresh horse. She pulled him to his feet and helped him mount.

"I think I'm going to pass out," Seiko said. Aderes smiled, and the horse shifted nervously as Seiko leaned over its side and threw up.

"The horse knows the way," she said as she tied Seiko to the saddle. "You are headed for an outpost on the Sedrian border. Tell them you need to speak with Marlon. There's a letter for him in your saddlebag."

Seiko's head drooped as he fought to stay conscious.

She slapped his uninjured leg. "What did I just say?"

"Ow!" he cried out. "Border outpost. Talk to Marlon. Note in bag."

"Good enough. Now go. Kana's coming."

Aderes slapped the horse's rump and it broke into a trot.

# CHAPTER 2

*How much does the boy know?*

Marlon sat in his office staring at reports from all over the world. Most were routine status updates. These he put into a pile to go through later. A knock sounded at his door and he looked up, expecting a page to add more reports to his stack.

"Come in."

A scout entered the room and closed the door behind him. The man had clearly been riding hard to reach the castle but had taken the time to change his clothes and wash his face before reporting to the Raven's office.

"What is it?" Marlon asked, intrigued, as the man stepped further into the office.

"Raven." The man saluted then continued. "A dragon rode into our Ijlala border outpost yesterday morning."

Marlon shot to his feet as the blood drained from his face. "How bad was the damage? Who was it?"

The scout shook his head and bowed. "Apologies, sir, I started in the middle. The outpost was undamaged when I left. The dragon's just a nine-year-old kid who keeps saying he needs to speak to you, sir."

"What did your captain do with him?" Marlon asked, relaxing slightly. "Where is he now?"

"He's been detained at the outpost. The captain didn't want to risk transporting him to the capitol in case he's not what he seems to be, and the outpost has been locked down to keep the news from spreading. The boy also had this letter in his saddlebag." The scout handed Marlon an envelope. "It's addressed to you. The captain thought it best to deliver it to you, unopened."

"Thank you," Marlon said, taking it from him. "Go to the kitchens and get something to eat, then report to the barracks and tell no one about the boy. We don't want to cause a panic."

"Yes, sir," the scout said as he saluted again, turned on his heel, and left.

Marlon sank into his chair and examined the envelope. The only thing on the front was his name in fashionable calligraphy. When he turned it over, he found that it was sealed with a drop of amber. He shook his head and broke the seal. "What lost puppy have you sent me now?"

*Raven,*

*I know you're concerned about this most recent refugee. His name is Seiko and, as I'm sure you've already deduced, he's Ryu's youngest son. I know there is no love lost between you and the Dragon King of Ijlal, but it is for that reason I have sent the boy to you. He is different from any dragon you have ever known, and his father wants him dead. Give the young prince a chance. You won't be disappointed.*

*Aderes, Enchantress of the Forest*

Marlon sighed and pocketed the letter as he returned to his house—although to call it a house was selling it short. It was the largest residential building outside the castle proper, a two-story rectangular wooden building with an impressive garden out back.

"Hello, love," his wife said with a smile as Marlon walked into the kitchen. She had white-blond hair that fell past her shoulders and pale blue eyes. She wore a full-length skirt and a light, long-sleeved shirt that hung loose on her thin frame. Marlon smiled and kissed her cheek. "You're home early," she observed.

He sighed, resting his hand on her back. "I've got an early start tomorrow."

She looked up at him, brow furrowed. "What's going on? You only just got back."

He pulled Aderes' letter out of his pocket and handed it to her.

She scanned it quickly, lips parted in surprise. "A dragon. Marlon, is she sure about this?"

He wrapped his arms around her, kissing her head. "We've never known her to be wrong. I need to see just who this kid is and help him if I can."

She closed her eyes and took a long, slow breath. "I know, and I trust your judgment. Just…be careful. If it is a trap, it's pretty sophisticated for Ryu, but you know firsthand the kind of destruction a dragon, even a young one, is capable of."

His arms tightened around her. "I promise."

*     *     *

He rode out early the next morning with four guards and a scout. They took their time getting to the outpost. Marlon didn't necessarily want to frighten the boy, but he promised his wife he'd be careful, and he needed to make sure the other outposts were prepared in the event this was a trap. It was a full week before Marlon and his group reached the outpost.

There was a commotion on the walls as the soldiers realized who was approaching their outpost. Marlon smiled to himself. Their reaction reminded him of the days when his mother returned from shopping and he hadn't done his chores yet. Regardless, these were well-trained soldiers who shouldn't have been caught off guard by his presence—or anything else, for that matter. He quickly composed his features as he dismounted and the captain approached him.

"Raven, we expected your arrival days ago," the captain said as he saluted.

Marlon turned to face him as his horse was led away. "What difference does that make?"

"None, sir," he said, trying not to fidget under Marlon's gaze.

Marlon shifted his gaze to the outpost itself. "Show me the defenses."

The captain turned and led Marlon up onto the outpost wall.

"What has Ryu been doing since his son ran away?" Marlon asked.

"Kana and his soldiers have been searching for the boy since he fled," the captain said, gesturing to a dark speck in the sky. "Kana has stayed well away from our border and out of range of our catapults, but our scouts report that the soldiers have ventured closer."

"Do they know we have him?"

The captain shook his head. "From what we've been able to gather, they believe that even had the dragon prince come to us, we would have either killed him ourselves or returned him to his father."

"I'm not surprised. It is in Ryu's best interest for his people to fear us as much as they fear him. How much does the boy know?"

"We try to keep him inside when Kana is visible in the sky, and we haven't told him what his father is doing, but his age is deceptive. He's smart enough to know that Ryu is searching for him. More than that, I think he's still afraid of what we might do to him."

Marlon looked up at the clear sky. "Where is he now?"

"Once his leg healed, we put him to work helping the stable-boys. Mostly feeding and mucking out stalls. I didn't think it was wise to trust him with anything more until you arrived."

"And how has he performed?" Marlon asked, interested.

The captain shrugged. "Better than I had anticipated, honestly. He's a hard worker who doesn't complain and does more than his fair share of the work. He's making the other boys look bad, and he's not even getting paid."

Marlon coughed, hiding a smile. "Bring him to your office. I want to talk to him."

The captain saluted.

# CHAPTER 3

*Everything is a test.*

Seiko entered the mess hall, waiting in line for his dinner. It was a large room located in the middle of the outpost and was where everyone came for their meals. Tables and benches were set up in four straight rows down its length. Seats weren't necessarily assigned but it was accepted practice that you sat with the people you worked with. Seiko sat down between two of the stablehands, laughing as one of them finished a joke.

One of them grinned. "Better eat fast, dragon. I hear Lynx is looking for you," he said, referring to the fort's captain.

Seiko ate quickly. That nickname, "dragon," while not original, didn't bother him. He felt no animosity in these boys.

"Too late," one of the other boys commented.

Seiko looked up from his dinner to see the captain enter the room and head straight for him. He felt his gut clench and he pushed his plate away, suddenly not hungry.

Everyone at the table fell silent as the captain stopped beside him. "Come with me," he said as he headed for the door.

Seiko rose and followed him, heart pounding.

When they reached the captain's office, the man opened the

door, gesturing for Seiko to enter. Seiko glanced quickly around the room. The only light came from a lamp on the edge of the desk. The corners of the room were engulfed in shadow. There was a thin bookshelf against the wall to Seiko's left, and various melee weapons were organized in the weapons rack on the wall to his right. The only other piece of furniture in the room was a chair that sat opposite the desk.

Seiko jumped as the door shut behind him with the captain still outside. With a start, he realized there was a man seated at the desk. "What's your name, boy?" the man asked.

"Seiko," he replied slowly. "But you already knew that. Who are you?"

The man sat back in the chair, studying Seiko. "Who do you think I am?"

"Is this a test?" Seiko asked.

A faint smile flashed across the man's face. "Everything is a test."

Seiko took his time studying the man. It was hard to tell since he was seated and the lighting was poor, but he didn't appear to be very tall. He was lean with a perfectly trimmed goatee and piercing ice-blue eyes. He wore no armor, at least not in the classical sense, although the leather he wore would afford him some protection and allow him to move unhindered. Embossed on both shoulder guards was a raven's head. The man had multiple daggers attached to straps on his torso, and Seiko knew there were probably many more that he couldn't see.

Finally, Seiko spoke. "I haven't seen you before, and I don't recognize the insignia on your shoulders. That places you outside the standing army. Your bearing is similar, though, and these men clearly defer to you, so you must exist in a capacity that supports this army and is probably integral to its survival."

"What makes you say that?" the man asked, head cocked to one side.

Seiko snorted. "You kicked the captain out of his own office and made him come get me. You're not just integral to this army. On some level, they fear you. You're a high-ranking intelligence officer, aren't you?"

The man grinned as he sat back in the chair, hands on the armrests. "I am Marlon Kasun, Raven of the Kingdom of Sedria."

Seiko's eyes widened and he clasped his hands together to keep them from shaking.

"I see you've heard of me by title, if not by name," Marlon observed.

"Ghost stories," the boy whispered.

"I'm sorry?"

Seiko took a deep breath and raised his eyes to meet Marlon's gaze. "In Ijlal, you're a ghost story. A myth. The thing we make up stories about to scare each other."

Marlon leaned forward, eyes bright. "Ghost stories like what?"

Seiko's initial fear was fading. This man didn't appear at all the way the stories painted him. "They call you Argus, the All-Seeing. They say you killed the Acamarian emperor and ate his heart. The stories claim that you are Zagreus' champion, the bringer of death."

"Stories to frighten children and spread to keep the people in line," Marlon mused. "But tell me, what does your father think of these…ghost stories?"

Seiko licked his suddenly dry lips. "Well, he's never actively supported their spread, but dragons are superstitious by nature, and as far as I know, he's never referred to you by name. He'd never admit to so base a feeling as fear, but I have no other name to give it."

Marlon laughed, startling Seiko. "Relax, boy, and sit down. I am not a monster any more than you are."

Seiko slowly sat in the chair across from Marlon, biting his lip, his short legs swinging in the air.

"I've been told you ran away because your father tried to kill you," Marlon said. Seiko looked away, shoulders tense. "Why? What does that gain him? From everything I've seen and heard of you so far, you're an intelligent, hard-working, capable young man who's willing to do dirty jobs without complaint, and charismatic enough that you've already begun to win over the people around you. Those are rare and very valuable traits."

Seiko shook his head with a rueful smile. "None of that is terribly meaningful to my father. He's more interested in savage cruelty and taking what he wants by force. He terrorizes his own civilians on a whim."

"Still, why kill his own son?"

Seiko looked down at his hands. "I don't agree with my father's methods or reasoning. I opposed him one too many times, I guess, so he tested me. He ordered me to execute a farmer who had done nothing wrong. I refused, so he locked me in the tower. I escaped before he decided how he wanted to kill me."

Marlon's eyes narrowed as he studied the boy. "Why not go along with him, as your brother so clearly does? The farmer was going to die whether or not you performed the act. It would have been far less dangerous for you to simply obey."

Seiko shook his head, remembering his last interaction with Kana. "My brother is a dragon by nature and enjoys indiscriminate violence."

"That's an interesting choice of phrase. You don't consider yourself a dragon?"

The boy hesitated. "I do not consider myself to be like them. I don't know what that means. All I know is that my father must be stopped, and I…would like to help."

Marlon studied him for a long moment. "You don't speak like a nine-year-old," he finally said.

Seiko shrugged. "When your only friends are stuffy old books and training dummies…"

"They told me you were injured when you arrived," Marlon said.

"That's correct. I broke my leg during my escape."

"Are you sure it was broken? You didn't limp in here, and it's only been a week."

Seiko shrugged. "Dragons heal fast."

Marlon rose to his feet, groaning as his back protested. "We leave in the morning."

Seiko followed suit, startled and afraid. "Where are we going?"

"After a conversation like that, I can't very well leave you to spend the rest of your life mucking out horse stalls, now, can I?" He smiled down at the boy. "We're going to the capitol. Let's see how much of your childhood we can save and give you a chance to be something other than the monster your father tried to turn you into."

Seiko jumped up from his chair and bowed. "Thank you, sir. I promise you won't regret giving me this chance."

Marlon grew serious. "It won't be easy. In fact, I cannot imagine a more difficult path you could have chosen," he warned. "There are many who will never trust a dragon, no matter what you do or how many lives you save. And the nature of a position such as mine is that most will never know the true extent of your sacrifice. There will be days when you'll wish your only responsibility was a few horses and their stalls, but if you choose to come with me, I promise you will make a difference, and maybe someday, you will be the ghost and I will be but a legend."

"That is everything I want, sir."

"Get some rest. It's going to be a long trip," he warned.

Seiko left the room, giddy.

Marlon closed his eyes and ran a hand through his hair, letting out a deep breath. "I'm sorry, Hannah, but this boy needs us. I cannot trust his fate to another. I know this will test you far more than me. Forgive me, my love," he said to the empty room before following his own advice and going to sleep.

# CHAPTER 4

*This is what safe feels like.*

Marlon rode into the castle courtyard with Seiko mounted behind him. As they dismounted, Seiko felt the hairs on the back of his neck stand up; he was being watched. He followed Marlon into the antechamber, palms sweating. Marlon and the soldiers had accepted him quickly, but he was all too aware of the devastation dragons had inflicted on these people.

"Wait here," Marlon ordered as he motioned to the guards and stepped into the audience chamber.

Seiko flinched as the doors shut with a loud clang. He craned his neck to look up at the giant golden-armored, halberd-wielding guards glaring down at him. He carefully stepped away from them and looked around the antechamber.

It was shaped like a hexagon with decorative columns spaced evenly from the main door that led from the courtyard to the entrance of the audience chamber. There were several smaller doors strategically hidden in the shadows of the columns that Seiko figured must have led to areas of the castle where the servants worked.

On one of the walls was a great tapestry that stretched from floor to ceiling and had been meticulously woven. Seiko moved to study it while still keeping an eye on the audience chamber door.

The tapestry depicted a scene straight out of legend. It was the only battle of the Invasion of Sedria by the Acamarian Empire. It had only been eleven years but already the battle had achieved a mythic status as a clash between warring gods and their champions.

On the right side of the tapestry, the Sedrian army was arrayed on the hillside. On the left, Acamar's soldiers stood in front of their ships, having just made landfall. The two armies clashed in the center of the tapestry where the sand met the foothills. On a hill overlooking the battlefield stood the Sedrian king in glittering, golden armor.

In the center of the melee crouched a giant, flaming salamander. Scattered around the monster were the burned, discarded corpses of Acamarian soldiers who had dared to fight him. This, then, was Sedria's Ruby Salamander, the Wolf to Marlon's Raven.

Seiko tore his gaze away from the salamander and found a lone ship anchored just offshore with a man standing confidently at the bow, hands clasped behind his back. Seiko recognized him as the emperor of Acamar by his swirling blue cape. Lurking in the shadow of the ship's mast crouched the cowled, scythe-wielding figure of Zagreus' most powerful servant, Argus the All-Seeing. The Grim Reaper.

Seiko felt a chill roll down his spine at the image. *That is the man you have chosen to trust?* he thought, gaze locked on the figure of Argus. *Zagreus' champion? The man who literally ate the heart of the last emperor of Acamar?*

He heard whispering and spun quickly, eyes wide, and came face to face with a girl no older than five.

"Be careful, Joy," Seiko heard someone whisper. It was the voice of a boy.

The little girl ignored the warning of the boy hiding behind her. "I'm Jocelynn," she said to Seiko. "What's your name?"

As Seiko looked at her, he felt a grin spread across his face. The little girl had long red hair tied in a tight ponytail. She had emerald green eyes, an open, smiling face sprayed with freckles, and she wore no shoes. Her clothes were expensive but clearly didn't belong to her. For one thing, they were too big for her. For another, Seiko was fairly certain her pants were being held up by a makeshift rope belt.

"I am called Seiko, my lady," he said with a graceful bow.

Jocelynn giggled. "Tarik, come here. He's not scary at all, and his manners are way better than yours."

The boy approached grudgingly, hands in his pockets. He was a few years older than the girl. He had short, dirty-blond hair, full lips, and a pale face. His eyes narrowed as he studied Seiko.

Glancing between them, Seiko realized whose closet the girl's clothes must have come from.

"Good manners doesn't mean he's harmless. He's a dragon," Tarik said.

"Do you really think Uncle Marlon would have brought him here and left him alone if he was a threat?" Jocelynn asked, eyes shining. "Where's your sense of adventure?"

"I left it upstairs with your clothes."

"So, what are you doing here?" Jocelynn asked, smiling at Seiko. "I can't remember the last time a dragon walked these halls."

"He is here because he has nowhere else to go and we are not in the habit of turning away refugees," a gruff voice said as an intimidating, broad-shouldered man in a red coat strode over, glaring at the children. "Your mother has been searching for you, and I have better things to do with my time than retrieve two wayward royals."

Seiko felt his legs start to shake as he stared up at Sedria's Ruby Salamander. True to his office, the Ruby Salamander wore a blood-red overcoat with a black breastplate and black pants. He wore steel-plated greaves that covered his knees, and embossed wolves' heads were stamped on his coat's shoulders. He had short-cropped black hair with a shock of gray at his left temple, and there was a scar across the right side of his face.

Tarik's face drained of color, but Jocelynn appeared unimpressed. She turned toward Seiko with a grin. "Hey, do you want to—"

The Ruby Salamander cleared his throat and glared at her, arms folded across his chest. "I see you're still stealing your brother's clothes."

She shrugged. "Can't climb trees in a dress."

"You shouldn't be climbing much of anything, princess. Go see your mother. She's waiting for you in her room."

"Fine," she grumbled as she headed for the stairs. Before she reached them, she stopped, turned around, and stuck her tongue out at him before running up the stairs, giggling.

"Joy!" Tarik called, exasperated, running after her.

The Ruby Salamander shook his head and strode away, ignoring Seiko, who stood in shock until Marlon returned twenty minutes later.

*       *       *

Seiko followed Marlon outside as the sun was setting. He looked up as Marlon led him through a gate and his mouth fell open. It was the largest house he'd ever seen—a huge two-story building made entirely out of wood.

"Seiko," Marlon called.

Seiko followed him inside, trembling. The house seemed even larger once he was inside. The foyer ceiling arched high over his head with a stained-glass window positioned to catch the light of the setting sun. The centerpiece of the window was a large raven, wings outstretched. Surrounding the bird were large, iridescent sunflowers that refracted the light, sparkling onto the far wall.

"Is that a fountain I hear out back?" Seiko whispered, eyes wide.

Marlon smiled and gently guided Seiko into the kitchen, where a woman looked up from the supper she was preparing. She was petite with white-blond hair and blue eyes. She wore a floor-length yellow dress with long sleeves. "Welcome home, darling," she said with a smile as Marlon kissed her cheek.

Seiko looked away, scuffing the toe of his boot against the wood floor. He glanced up quickly as the woman began to cough.

Once her coughing subsided, Marlon handed her a glass of water that had been sitting on the counter. She took a sip then set the glass down and turned to Seiko. "This is the boy you told me about?"

Seiko looked at Marlon, wondering what he'd told her.

"Yes, love. This is Seiko." Marlon smiled. "Seiko, this is my wife, Hannah."

Seiko bowed wordlessly, mouth suddenly dry. He had gotten very good at reading people. It had saved his life on more than one occasion, and he knew just by looking that Marlon would do anything for his wife. Her opinion mattered more to Marlon than even the king's, and she was Ijlala. Seiko feared that she had already made up her mind about him.

"Why flee from your own father?" she asked Seiko.

"My father kills and tortures people on a whim. What he does is wrong, and I can't watch him hurt and kill the innocent," Seiko answered slowly.

"You are a very brave young man," Hannah said. "The first room on your left at the top of the stairs is yours if you want to lie down for a bit. Supper will be ready shortly."

Seiko bit his lip, frozen in place, eyes darting around the room.

"Seiko," Hannah said softly as she slowly approached. He looked up at her, eyes wide, panting. She knelt in front of him, tears in her eyes. "Seiko, you're safe here."

"I…don't even know what that would feel like," he said, suddenly sounding very young.

Hannah pulled him gently into her arms, ready to release him if he fought her. He was stiff, trapped between fight and flight, but he allowed her to hold him.

"This is what safe feels like," she whispered as her tears fell onto his neck. "Ryu is powerful and cruel and his reach is long, but you are safe here. He cannot reach here, not into this house."

Seiko buried his face in her neck and his shoulders shook as he sobbed, his little hands clinging to her dress. When he was finished, Hannah released him and rose to her feet.

"The fountain?" Seiko asked, rubbing his eyes.

"It's straight through the back door if you want to check it out," Marlon said.

Seiko turned and headed back toward the foyer.

"Stars, Hannah, I love you," Marlon breathed as he wrapped his arms around her waist.

She smiled and kissed his cheek.

*       *       *

Seiko left the house and stopped, staring at the garden. In the center was a beautiful, delicate fountain. In concentric circles around it were arranged flowerbeds bursting with color. Next to the house was a small herb and vegetable garden, and the outer walls were covered in vines and sunflowers. The mix of perfumes was heady. He walked to the fountain and leaned against it. The sound of the fountain proved too much for the exhausted dragon. He yawned and closed his eyes.

*      *      *

"Seiko," a voice called as a hand touched his arm.

Seiko rolled over, lashing out with his foot. Marlon skipped back, watching the boy carefully. Seiko looked around, regaining his bearings. "Sorry, Argus."

Marlon shrugged, lips twitching. "You're not the first skittish orphan we've taken in. Come on. Hannah says supper's ready."

Seiko rose and followed Marlon into the dining room. As they began to eat, Seiko would periodically glance up at Hannah and then quickly away whenever she looked at him.

Finally, she set her utensils on the table and folded her hands in her lap. "Seiko?" She waited until he looked at her. "What is it?"

He looked down, unsure if there was a polite way to voice his question. "You're Ijlala."

She smiled sadly. "Is it still my accent?"

"That and…" He pointed to his plate. "You learned to make this in Ijlal. I would guess from your mother?"

She smiled. "Well, you're not wrong."

"How did an Ijlala end up in Sedria married to Argus, of all people?"

"I grew up in Ijlal as the youngest daughter of a farming clan. We were not wealthy, but somehow my father always managed to scrape together enough gold to appease Ryu. Seventeen years ago, there was a severe drought and the ground was too parched to yield a good crop." Hannah shook her head at the memory. "My father used every farming trick he knew to try and coax production from that barren field. As harvest season drew to a close, he traveled to the capitol to plead our case. He never returned. A few nights later, our fields, livestock, barn, and house were set ablaze by dragon fire."

Seiko stared as she began coughing uncontrollably, realizing what must have caused such extensive damage to her lungs. When she could breathe normally, Marlon offered her a glass of water.

Hannah took a sip before smiling sadly at Seiko and continuing her story. "My family burned to death in that fire. I only survived because I was down in the cellar. Hours later, after hearing my family screaming and suffering severe burns and smoke inhalation myself, I emerged from the cellar scared and traumatized. No one would help me for fear of the dragon's wrath being turned on them. Lost and alone, I eventually wandered into the forest to die, but I was aided by Aderes, the guardian of the forest, who guided me to a Sedrian outpost."

"An outpost I was currently supervising," Marlon said, taking up the narrative as he took another sip of water. "She stumbled in scared, dehydrated, and malnourished with burns all over her body. She was met with suspicion and scorn. But she weathered it all with a stately grace that still amazes me."

She rolled her eyes. "And then I fainted."

Marlon chuckled. "And then she fainted, and we were immediately ashamed of our actions. We treated her injuries as best we could, and by the end of the week, she had us all eating out of her hand."

"Well, not everyone," she reminded him, nudging him with her shoulder.

He shrugged. "You were an enigma, and I was in awe of your

strength. I still am."

"Then how did you two end up together?" Seiko asked.

Hannah laughed. "There is no denying what the Watchers have decreed."

"We found another Ijlala refugee about a week later. My men wanted to kill him," Marlon said. "Hannah stood up to them and, I think, shocked us all. The two of us started talking after that. She wanted to help her people, and I wanted to steal as much from Ryu as possible. Aysel, Aderes' daughter, found us soon after and offered to help. Between the three of us, we set up a program to help assimilate any refugees that can reach us into Sedrian society. And the more time I spent with Hannah, the more I was drawn to her strength and compassion."

"For my part," Hannah continued, "I felt the safest place I could be was in the presence of the one person Ryu feared: the Raven of Sedria. That self-preservation instinct eventually gave way to friendship, and finally, love."

Marlon pressed her hand to his lips. "Aderes and Aysel help orphans and refugees reach our borders then I ride out to assess their state of mind and any potential security risks."

"Then he brings them here and I help them adjust, find work and a home."

"But why help me?" Seiko asked, looking at Hannah. "I'm not just some helpless, wounded child. I'm a dragon, and my father murdered your whole family. That you didn't share their fate was a fluke, not a choice. My father doesn't spare people."

Hannah reached across the table for Seiko's hand. He blinked, seeing the burn scars up and down her arm. She smiled gently and placed her hand on top of his.

"Seiko, you are not a monster. You are a child who chose to do the right thing in a difficult situation. I don't care that you're Ryu's son any more than I care that the local baker is from Acamar. You are welcome in my house for as long as you choose to stay."

Seiko looked from one to the other and back again. "Excuse me," he said as he fled upstairs.

"Let him go," Hannah said as Marlon rose. "He needs time to process. Compassion is not something he's used to."

*       *       *

Seiko tossed and turned, unable to sleep. The bed was too soft, the house too quiet, and he half expected it to burst into flame at any moment. He began to shake as fear and panic rose to the surface. He heard murmuring from downstairs. He got out of bed and crept toward the landing.

"You mean this to be longer than just a few days to find him a permanent home," Hannah said.

Marlon sighed. "I don't really know who I could trust to take in a dragon child, but I need to know that you're with me. People already don't trust you because of your origins. To raise a dragon fleeing from Ijlal, Ryu's own son… You are the strongest person I know, but I know what I'm asking. The decision is yours, love."

"I need you to tell me why, Marlon," she said. "You will face your own consequences for this. What is it about this one out of all the refugees we've helped that makes you want to raise him? Who knows what Ryu will do when he realizes what's happened?"

"He's a dragon and Ryu's son. Keeping him close gives us an advantage we've never had before, and we need every advantage we can get."

"That's the answer you gave Kolya, but that's not the whole answer."

Marlon chuckled. "You're right. The boy is *good*, Hannah. He wants to do the right thing, to help people. We've always assumed that Ryu corrupts everything he touches, but not this boy, his own son! There will be those who demand his execution merely for the fault of his parentage. No one should be raised in that hell, but he has emerged kind. I want him to feel safe, and I want to show him that he can make a difference. He needs to know that being a monster is a choice and not a product of your lineage."

"Kolya would have said you're getting soft." Hannah paused, thinking. "He may stay, but you need to make sure if he chooses to stand against Ryu that it's his choice. That boy has already seen enough violence for a lifetime."

"I love you," he said softly.

Seiko returned to his room, lost in thought.

# CHAPTER 5


*I'm not a monster.*

As the months passed, Seiko settled into a regimented routine. He had weapons practice in the morning with a group of highborn boys around his age. Afterward, he went home for lunch with Hannah and Marlon, assuming the Raven of Sedria wasn't on a trip and hadn't gotten distracted by work. Then it was back out to the yard for mounted combat training. Once this was over, he would go to Marlon's office for lessons on politics and statecraft. Once evening came, he would return home for supper and sleep. Seiko had acclimated so well that, for the first time in his life, he was able to sleep soundly without wondering if he would be stabbed or poisoned.

This wasn't to say he was universally accepted. But with the acceptance of King Auren and the protection of living under Marlon's roof, he was safe from physical assault...or so he thought.

One night as they finished supper, Marlon smiled at Seiko. "Seek, we need to talk. Come on."

Seiko glanced at Hannah, who smiled and squeezed his hand. He rose and followed Marlon out to the garden.

"Hannah and I have decided that we would like to formally

adopt you," Marlon said without preamble.

Seiko's eyes widened. That they had chosen to open their home to him was a kindness and a blessing, but this... "Why?"

Marlon cocked his head. "That's an odd response, but I suppose it's fair. As I'm sure you are aware, being a dragon in Sedria puts you in a potentially dangerous situation. Many of the people here hate dragons indiscriminately, and we are far enough removed from Ryu's presence that some of them may choose to act on that hatred. They see only the vulnerable child of the dragon who destroyed their lives."

"What does any of that have to do with you?"

Marlon smiled. "The most reliable way to keep that from happening is to attach you to my family. It would give everyone a very real, close threat to deter them from taking their anger out on you."

"And?"

"What?"

"That you've already accomplished. Why adopt me?"

"Hannah and I have thus far been unable to have children of our own. You are everything we could have wished for in a son." He hesitated. "I'm also hoping to use you against your father."

"I can't let you do that," Seiko said slowly.

"Which part?"

"I don't care about you using me against my father," Seiko clarified. "I ran away from him because what he's doing is wrong. But I can't let you adopt me. My father would not rest until your entire family is dead."

Marlon shrugged. "He already hates me."

Seiko shook his head as his hands balled into fists. "You don't understand. He wants to kill me. If you do this, you'll be placing yourself and Hannah between me and him. My father doesn't go around obstacles. He annihilates them."

"You're worried about Hannah," Marlon realized.

Seiko dipped his head. "She doesn't need another target on her back."

"Strength comes in many forms, Seek, and compassion is not a weakness. Ryu placed a bounty on me and Hannah years ago. He's been trying to kill me for years and he's welcome to try again, but there is a reason your father fears me. My reputation is not all smoke, mirrors, and rumor. The tapestry in the castle foyer is not unfounded propaganda. I did earn the title of Argus."

"I still don't think it's a good idea," Seiko said, biting his lip. "But if you decide to do it anyway, I would be forever grateful. There's just one thing…"

"What is it?"

"I don't think I could ever call you 'father.' It's just not a word I associate with positive things in my life. Do you mind If I keep calling you Argus?"

Marlon chuckled. "I don't mind at all."

Seiko smiled in relief.

*     *     *

Weeks later, Seiko was headed home from weapons class in the training yard when something hard glanced off his shoulder. He ducked his head on instinct then looked up to see a passel of boys had gathered around him while he'd been lost in thought. A few of them held fist-sized rocks in their hands, leering at him.

"Dragon boy," one of the older boys taunted. "Murderer."

Seiko straightened, looking at the boys surrounding him. Some were in his classes, but most weren't. He knew they were parroting the hateful things they'd heard from their parents and elders. These kids had not lived through vicious dragon attacks, and they didn't really care about him. They were just bullies looking for a fight.

"You want me to attack you," he said to them. "I won't give you the satisfaction. I'm not the monster your parents think I am."

One of the boys stepped up and punched him in the stomach. "Coward," he spat as Seiko doubled over, gasping for breath.

"I won't fight you," Seiko said through clenched teeth as the boy punched him again, causing him to fall to the ground. The boy extended his leg, and the rest began to close in. Seiko shut his eyes tight, curling into a ball, but the blow never landed.

He heard scuffling and surprised cries as fabric brushed against his face. Seiko opened his eyes as the boy who had hit him staggered to his feet, the entire group shifting back uneasily. Inches from his face, Seiko saw soft boots and a skirt. He looked up. Hannah.

She stood between him and his attackers, posture rigid and eyes ablaze. At the sight of her face, Seiko's breath caught in his throat. This was not a calculated act designed to win his trust. This was a furious mother bear willing to fight to the death against impossible odds for her son.

"Do not touch him," she warned. "Such barbaric actions are not tolerated in Sedria. Your parents and your mentors will be informed."

Seiko looked at her in surprise and admiration. His father had always said that humans were weak cowards, no better than scavengers. Human in general and Hannah specifically had never seemed very strong to him. It had always baffled him that Ryu had lost to a bunch of humans. In that moment, lying helpless on the ground behind Hannah, Seiko began to realize that strength was not always a physical characteristic. Sometimes, it was the courage to stand tall and weather the storm. Hannah had thrown herself between him and his attackers with no thought for her safety. She did not need his protection, and it was arrogant for him to assume otherwise.

"Lady, I know you can't have kids," the leader of the gang of boys sneered as a few of his friends chuckled. "But are you really so desperate that you're going to claim that thing as your child? It's not even human."

"Species is irrelevant," she snapped, helping Seiko to his feet. "He is my son and will be treated as such unless you would like a visit from the Raven."

"Yes, ma'am," they all muttered, faces pale.

She glared as they fearfully bowed to her and ran. Then she turned to Seiko. "Are you alright?"

"Sorry about the laundry," he said quietly, realizing she had dropped her basket when she'd raced to help him.

She waved her hand dismissively. "It can be washed again."

"Where are you headed?" Seiko asked as he gathered up the clothes and placed them in the basket.

"Home." Gesturing to the basket, Hannah added, "I can carry that."

"I want to help," Seiko said with a smile. "Mom."

She hugged him.

*       *       *

Seiko took a deep breath as he left his house and headed for his training session in the yard. After his beating from the day before, he wasn't sure what to expect. He heard someone calling his name and he turned toward the sound, tense. He could still feel the bruises on his shoulder and ribs.

"Your Highness?" he gasped in surprise.

Being of similar age, Tarik was in most of his classes, but the two boys had never spoken. Tarik made a face as he stopped beside Seiko. "Just call me Tarik unless I'm wearing that stupid crown."

"Very well, Tarik," Seiko said with a bow that made the other boy roll his eyes. "Is there something I can help you with?"

Tarik shoved his hands into his pockets and began walking toward the practice arena. Seiko fell into step beside him.

"I heard about what happened yesterday," Tarik said. "I wasn't part of the group that attacked you, and I didn't know what they were going to do, but I knew they were going to do something. I should have prevented it, and I didn't. I wanted to apologize and ask if maybe we could start over?"

"Fair enough, and I appreciate the apology."

Tarik smiled in relief.

# CHAPTER 6



*No more secrets.*

Marlon entered his house and kissed Hannah's cheek.

"How was your day?" she asked with a smile.

Before he could answer, there was a popping sound like a glass shattering against the floor. "Who else is here?" Marlon asked.

"Just Seiko," she answered. "He ran into the drawing room when he got home."

Marlon headed for the drawing room door, Hannah following. As he opened it, the sound came again, this time from the fireplace inside the room. Seiko looked up at Marlon, eyes wide.

"What's going on?" Marlon asked, watching him.

"Nothing, it's fine," Seiko said quickly, eyes darting around the room. "I just didn't get my block up fast enough during training."

"Let me see," Marlon ordered, wondering why the boy was being so cagey.

"It's fine, really. It's barely a scratch," Seiko said as he backed away, but Marlon was quicker, and he grabbed Seiko's elbow. "I said no!" Seiko yelled, tearing his arm from Marlon's grasp.

Marlon took a step after him, but the unmistakable stench of burning flesh filled the room. He turned his hand over and watched in horrified fascination as Seiko's silver blood ate a line from the middle of his forearm to the center of his palm. Marlon heard Hannah scream, then the pain hit him and he slid to his knees with a groan.

"No! No, no, no," Seiko shouted as he raced back to Marlon. "This is what I was trying to avoid." He pressed a clean cloth to the wound, gritting his teeth as it immediately began to corrode.

"The water pump outside!" Hannah said, one of Marlon's arms already slung across her shoulders. Seiko grabbed Marlon's other arm, and the two of them helped him outside.

"Keep it under the water," Seiko said as he worked the pump feverishly. Ten minutes later, shaking and sweating, he stopped pumping.

Hannah pressed the corner of her apron to Marlon's wound. Both she and Seiko smiled in relief when the cloth didn't immediately begin to corrode.

Seiko collapsed to the ground in exhaustion. "I guess you want to know what just happened."

Marlon was sweating and breathing heavily with his head resting against Hannah's chest. "But not tonight. We're all exhausted, son. We'll talk in the morning."

Seiko bit his lip as the three of them staggered into the house.

Once Marlon was bandaged and sleeping, Hannah turned to Seiko, who couldn't meet her gaze. "Are you alright?" she asked softly.

He looked up at the unexpected question, unshed tears in his eyes. Hannah knelt, and he clung to her as he sobbed. "I didn't mean to! He's…he's not going to die, is he?"

"Shh," Hannah whispered. "It would take a great deal more than that to kill a legend like Argus, son. Sleep, now. You are our son, and nothing you can say or do will change that."

Seiko wept and held on to Hannah tightly.

*       *       *

Seiko woke in the morning and dressed quickly but couldn't bring himself to open the door and walk downstairs. He chewed his lip as he glanced at the window, wondering how much the fall would hurt and if Marlon would even bother to look for him. Hannah's words kept him from taking that option. He had chosen this family, and what had happened had been his fault. He would stay and bear whatever punishment was deemed fitting for his crimes. Thus resolved, he opened his bedroom door and froze when he saw Marlon sitting in the hallway, waiting. He had dark circles under his eyes and a bandage wrapped around his arm to just below the elbow.

"May I come in?" Marlon asked.

Seiko bowed his head wordlessly and stepped to one side. Marlon entered the room and sat on the bed. After a few moments, Seiko followed suit, staring at his hands. They sat in silence for a long while. Seiko could feel Marlon's eyes on him.

Finally, he could take the silence no longer. "Are you alright?" Seiko asked, voice barely above a whisper.

Marlon sighed as he slowly unwound the bandages from his hand and forearm. "You gave me another scar to add to my collection, but I retained the use of my hand."

"I'm glad. I never meant to hurt you."

"I understand that it was an accident," Marlon said slowly, studying the boy. "But, Seek, you need to tell me what's going on."

Seiko wiped his nose on his sleeve as Marlon wound the bandage around his arm once more. "I'll try, but it doesn't make any more sense to me than it does to you. This is why my father wants to kill me. Kana stabbed me in the arm, and my blood just…kind of…ate the blade."

"You're ten years old and you're telling me that you've never bled before?" Marlon said in surprise.

"It's really not all that unusual for a dragon," Seiko said with a shrug. "We're hatched, not born, and we kind of…skip the awkward toddler phase. We have thicker skin than humans, and dragon's blood—well, *other* dragon's blood, anyway—combusts when it comes in contact with the air. We also have conscious control over our blood flow. We can control the rate of flow as well as how much we bleed, to an extent. I was warned very early on that bleeding would earn me a severe punishment contingent upon what the fire damaged."

Marlon shook his head. "It's still hard to imagine a child that doesn't know the color of his own blood at ten years old."

"I did have a few minor cuts and scrapes when I was younger, but none were deep enough to necessitate bleeding, so I just…didn't. I got cut yesterday during training. It was deep enough that I knew it would bleed, but not so deep that I couldn't delay it. I managed to get home before it started bleeding, but then Mom asked me how my day went, and my control slipped. I ran into the drawing room, but you came home just a few minutes after I did. I tried to stanch the flow with rags, but—"

"Your blood destroyed them."

"I didn't want to put them on the floor, so I threw them into the fireplace. Apparently, my blood shatters before it burns."

"Yeah, I heard that."

"So what happens now?" Seiko asked, finally looking at Marlon.

Marlon smiled and reached over to ruffle Seiko's hair. He froze as Seiko flinched away from him and then placed his hands in his lap. "I'm not going to hit you, son," he said softly.

Seiko opened his eyes, confused. "But I hurt you."

Marlon pulled him into a hug. "What happened was an accident and as much my fault as yours. I don't blame you, but no more secrets, okay? Not between us."

"Understood, Argus."

Marlon grunted as he rose to his feet. "Now, let's see what your mother has made for breakfast!"

*       *       *

As Seiko left for weapons practice, Hannah turned to Marlon. "You're troubled."

"Yes," he said. "He is unlike any dragon I have ever heard of."

"What does that mean?"

"I don't know, but considering who sent him to us, she must plan to use him for her own ends."

"He's just a child," Hannah said, frowning.

"I need to find out why he's different and what her plans are."

"You're headed into the forest."

He sighed. "Hopefully, Aysel will be forthcoming. If not… I may be gone all night."

*       *       *

"Aysel!" Marlon called as he entered a clearing deep within Aderes' forest.

"No need to shout, Argus. I am always here," a woman said, stepping from the shadows. She was tall with black hair that seemed to reflect the moonlight and form a halo around her. Other than the vines running down her arms and up her neck like veins, she looked like a normal woman. "How is the boy?"

"Seek is fine. What can you tell me about him?"

The woman cocked her head. "Let me see the burn."

Marlon unwrapped his arm, wincing as she examined it.

"The damage could have been much worse. What did you do?" she asked.

"He flushed it with water, but it was Hannah's idea."

"If it happens again, use sand first to remove the bulk of his blood. The finer the sand, the more efficiently it will act as a sponge and clump together, absorbing his silver blood. The saturated sand will combust, but it will be normal fire and will die quickly."

"Aysel, why is he different? What is it about his blood that caused Ryu to turn against his own son?" Marlon asked as she re-bandaged his arm.

"Ryu is not truly his father. Dragons hatch from eggs created by the stars. They are the foot soldiers in the eternal war between the celestial *zakyri* and the *zoren*, but he is no *akyrier*, not truly. We know him as Tukiko."

"Son of the moon?" Marlon asked.

"Jericho is *zoren*," she answered, glancing up at the moon. "He is your son's sire, in as far as a dragon can be said to have one. He is the moonsilver dragon, created to combat the others. Dragonsbane will not harm him. He is the dragon who is the dragon slayer."

"A dragon slayer," Marlon repeated. "You want my son to physically fight the dragons?"

"It is what he was born for, and he is our best weapon against them. Ryu knows this and that is why he turned on the boy."

"You have given me much to think on," Marlon said as he turned away.

"I have one more piece of information for you," Aysel called.

Marlon turned to look at her, on edge. Aysel very rarely offered information.

"His silver blood is one of the reasons he heals so quickly, even from a grievous injury, and it will burn a normal person, as you've discovered firsthand."

"But?" he prompted when she hesitated.

"Your Black Falcon. Should she choose to trust him, his blood can aid in her recovery."

"How? She is no dragon."

Aysel smiled. "She is apprenticed to the Ruby Salamander, and she is Malandran."

"She's not injured."

"No, but she will be. Or has your Wolf's training regimen been altered?"

Marlon shook his head. "Thank you for your help, Aysel."

"Always a pleasure, Argus," she said as he left, the clearing disappearing behind him.

# CHAPTER 7



*What you see is not always the truth.*

Seiko looked up from the family crests he was studying.

Marlon stood looking out the window, hands clasped behind his back. He turned and smiled when he saw Seiko watching him. "You have a question."

Seiko hesitated then shook his head.

"Ask the question, Seek," Marlon encouraged. It wasn't like the young dragon to hesitate.

"When we met, you told me that I am not a monster any more than you are. What did you mean by that?"

Marlon sat on the corner of his desk. "Why ask that question now? Do you believe yourself to be a monster?"

Seiko closed the book in front of him, thinking. "I suppose that depends on your definition of a monster."

"What I believe a monster to be should have no bearing on whether you believe yourself to be one. Words are funny things. They don't always mean the same thing to everyone. What is your definition of a monster?"

Seiko chewed his lip as he considered the question. "A monster is a cruel, savage being who hurts others for sport or his own selfish motivations," he finally said, watching Marlon's face. "A monster takes no heed to the lives he destroys to accomplish his goal."

"By that definition, do you believe yourself to be a monster?" Marlon asked, leaning forward.

Seiko shook his head.

Marlon sat back watching the boy. "I do not believe you're a monster, either. *Ser na'gire disa na'zdis zaler gire.*"

Seiko narrowed his eyes. "That was Mekan, right? What does it mean?"

"Your teachers tell me that, while you're not fluent, you are fairly proficient. Why don't you tell me what it means?"

"Can you repeat it?" Seiko asked, closing his eyes.

*"Ser na'gire disa na'zdis zaler gire,"* Marlon said slowly.

Seiko sat with his eyes closed, lips moving as he murmured the phrase to himself. At last, he opened his eyes and asked, "Monsters are made by choice?"

Marlon smiled. "Close. Our existence doesn't make us monsters, our choices do. A dragon doesn't have to be a savage beast, and humans don't have to act humanely. Eventually, your choices reveal who and what you truly are, not the skin you wear. The people who label you a monster merely for the fact of your birth are the same small-minded people who would call me a monster because they will not or cannot understand my actions."

"Are you really who they say you are?" Seiko asked. "Argus the All-Seeing? Did you really eat the heart of the emperor of Acamar?"

Marlon chuckled. "That is a title I was given after Acamar's attempted invasion. What do you know about the original myth of Argus—not how it pertains to me?"

"Well, Argus was a great warrior who impressed the god-queen

Pasiphae so much that she made him her personal champion, but her husband became jealous. To save her lover, Pasiphae gifted Argus to her twin brother, Zagreus, the god of death and punisher of broken oaths. Argus' martial ability and loyalty quickly made him one of Zagreus' favored lieutenants. For a thousand years, Argus served death faithfully and there was peace between the gods. Although Argus was now immortal, his soul was human still, and he longed to return to the land of the living. Zagreus was not unsympathetic to his champion's heart, so he devised a compromise: he would return Argus to the land of the living as Death's avatar with the onus to correct the imbalances created by Pasiphae. This displeased her greatly to have her gift turned against her, but she had no recourse. For how does one kill a servant of Death itself?"

"And what does your father say about me?"

Seiko rose and moved toward the bookcase, brows knit. "I don't believe he has ever uttered the term 'Argus.' He pretends the rumors don't exist. My father believes you to be the physical manifestation of the Grim Reaper, the ultimate dealer of death to oath breakers and those who would extend their life beyond their appointed time. But what Ryu believes is not the same as the stories that run rampant through the villages of Ijlal. They say that Argus' original body has decayed and disappeared. He is now a spirit and must possess another's body to act. They say you are his most recent acquisition. That you drew his attention when you boarded the Acamarian emperor's ship, and that he possessed you, guiding your hand as you killed the emperor and ate his heart."

"But why?" Marlon asked, head cocked, a smile playing on his lips. "Why would Zagreus want the emperor of Acamar dead?"

"The stories claim that the goddess Pasiphae had upset the balance by refusing to relinquish the emperor's soul to Zagreus at the appointed time."

"According to Acamarian beliefs, their emperor has never truly died because his heart was always consumed by the next emperor. But I didn't end the cycle; I perpetuated it. I ate his heart, or so the Acamarians believe."

"True you didn't technically end the cycle," Seiko said slowly. "But as a servant of Zagreus, you have stolen Acamar from Pasiphae, provided one of her servants doesn't eat your heart." Seiko cocked his head and walked over to Marlon. "But what's the truth? What really happened?"

"The Acamarians do not believe me to be Argus, as their myth is somewhat different, but they do believe me to be a servant of Zagreus. I did eat their emperor's heart. When Acamar's generals realized what had happened, they sent their champions against me."

"Why not challenge you themselves?"

"Acamar's generals pledge their undying loyalty to their emperor. Since I had eaten his heart, they were barred from challenging me. I killed their champions and ordered them to return home."

"So what really happened that day?" Seiko asked. "I mean, I've seen the tapestry and heard the stories, but…"

"The tapestry in the castle foyer is an accurate depiction albeit with a poetic spin," Marlon said. "I did not and never have physically manifested as the Grim Reaper. Kolya can summon the Ruby Salamander armor, but he cannot control fire. King Auren was there, but we didn't leave him on a hill in gaudy golden armor—that's just stupid. Between my scouts and Queen Phaedra's spies, we knew Acamar was coming and were arrayed on the beach when they made landfall." He paused and turned away, clearing his throat. "Koyla and the army drew their attention while I swam out to the emperor's flagship. I slew the emperor and consumed his heart then ordered the ship's crew to beach it. Then I fought each of Acamar's champions, one after another. After I defeated them, Acamar's generals swore their loyalty to me. I ordered them to return home, and Acamar has been relatively quiet since then. From what we've been able to gather, the Acamarians believe there is a war being waged in the heavens between Pasiphae and Zagreus for control of Acamar and fate itself. Their shamans have advised no further action until the nature of the heavens is revealed."

"That's very…esoteric. What would that even look like?"

"I believe they are waiting for me to die," Marlon said with a shrug. "What that means for Sedria will depend a great deal on the circumstances surrounding my death."

"So…you ate his heart, like, literally tore it from his chest and swallowed it?"

Marlon chuckled. "Yes. Does that make me a monster?"

Seiko bit his lip, brow furrowed. "Why did you do it?"

Marlon rose and returned to looking out the window, hands once again clasped behind his back. "What do you know about Acamar?"

"They have a strict caste system with the shamans and triumvirate at the top. The slaves are at the bottom, made up of conquered peoples and those born into it. They despise diplomacy, even viewing it as a sign of weakness. They'd never lost, never even backed down until they set their eyes on Sedria."

"And where does cardiophagia fit in their religion and culture?"

Seiko looked away, hands balled into fists. He didn't like it when he didn't have an answer.

Marlon sighed, turning from the window. "Of course your father wouldn't have bothered to explain the reasons; he may not even know himself. Acamarians believe in reincarnation, but that cannot happen while one's heart is sustaining another."

"So they eat hearts to gain another's courage and postpone that person's reincarnation," Seiko said.

Marlon smiled encouragingly. "And not just enemies. Children will eat their parents' hearts. It is the ultimate sign of respect, so they only eat the hearts of those they believe are somehow better than them. And it is how they determine succession. The new emperor is the one who consumes the previous emperor's heart, thus gaining the power of all the rulers that came before. They also believe that burning bodies is the ultimate desecration and the act of a coward."

"So you ate his heart and defeated Acamar's champions. Then what?"

"I ordered them to return home and trouble Sedria no further. They did so, and now the triumvirate rules in my stead. They have agents who are charged with retrieving my heart should I die unexpectedly. Having said all of that, do you believe me to be a monster?"

Seiko looked up at him. "No. It may have been gross, but it was necessary. Anything less would have resulted in Sedria's annihilation."

"I agree. Now, I have work to do. And I believe you have a tutor waiting for you."

Seiko's eyes widened and he headed for the door.

*       *       *

Hannah looked up from where she was kneading bread to see Seiko and Tarik enter the room, each carrying a stack of books.

"This is too much information," Tarik complained. "There's no way I'm going to remember it all."

They set their books on the kitchen table and Tarik dropped

heavily into a chair.

Seiko cocked his head. "Wait here."

Tarik looked up when Hannah set a glass of water next to him. "It all comes so easily to him," he said. "I feel dumb."

She smiled gently. "Everyone has their strengths and weaknesses. What you see is not always the truth."

Seiko reentered the room, and Hannah returned to her bread dough. "What happened at the Battle of Fallow Fields?" Seiko asked Tarik as he set a polished wooden box on the table between them.

Tarik stared at the box in Seiko's hands. "That battle happened during my great-grandfather's reign. Oslia had accused him of privateering and declared war. When he invaded, they burned their fields. The scars from that conflict remain. Though they are active trade partners, they are slow to trust."

"See? It's not that you can't remember this stuff."

Tarik shrugged. "Battles and history are easy. It's all the organizational details and diplomatic minutiae that trips me up."

"Minutiae, huh?" Seiko asked with a grin. "You have a great memory. You just need context."

"It's just so easy for you."

Seiko shrugged. "I remember lists and names but I can't pull every battle we've ever studied out of my head like you can." He opened the box and began to take pieces out of it.

Tarik looked up at him. "I don't have time to play chess," he snapped. "If I can't find a way to remember this stuff, Wolf will have my head."

"Relax, we're not playing," Seiko said with a smile as he took the pieces and lined them up in two rows, one black and one white. "Take a good look at the pieces."

Tarik looked at them, brow furrowed. "Boar, bear, wolf, stag lion, and lynx. What are you getting at?" His eyes widened in sudden realization. "Military ranks?"

Seiko looked up, smiling. "Chess was not designed as a civilian hobby. It was meant to teach young officers ranks, tactics, and logistics."

Tarik stared at the pieces, finger tracing the board as he tried to remember. "So if the white pieces are military ranks, does that make the black pieces intelligence ranks?"

"Right, and those ranks are?"

"Badger, Panther, Shark, Fox, Cobra, and Raven."

Seiko smiled. "Each officer's epaulets are stamped with the animal that corresponds to his or her rank. The exception, of course, being the Black Falcon. Wolf's apprentice has no face and no official rank. Now, what order do they go in? Lowest to highest rank."

"Boar, Bear, Lynx, Stag, Lion, and the Wolf is Kolya."

"Good. And what about intelligence ranks?"

Tarik rolled his eyes. "Badger, Panther, Shark, Cobra—"

"Wait, one of those is wrong," Seiko interrupted.

"Which one?"

"Cobra."

"Badger, Panther, Shark…Fox?" Tarik guessed.

"Good," Seiko said, gesturing for him to continue.

"Then Cobra, and the Raven is Marlon."

Seiko grinned. "See, you can do this. Let's try this: I'll give you a rank, and you have to tell me which animal it corresponds to."

"Alright," Tarik said softly, staring at the chess pieces before him.

"Major," Seiko said, watching him.

Tarik reached for the stag then hesitated, glanced at Seiko, and picked up the Lynx.

Seiko shook his head. "You were right the first time. Don't

second-guess yourself. Major is the stag. Second Lieutenant?"

Tarik paused then slowly picked up the boar.

Seiko smiled encouragingly "That's correct."

"Prince Tarik," a servant said, knocking at the door.

The boys looked at each other and returned to the front room.

"The king requests your presence in his study," the man said with a bow.

"Go on," Seiko said. "I'll clean this up and meet you for weapons practice."

"Thanks. I'll see you later."

"You were very patient with him," Hannah observed as the door closed behind Tarik and Seiko returned the chess pieces to the box.

"He gets frustrated quickly, but he's not stupid. If you come at the problem from the right angle, he picks it up right away."

"You sound a lot like your father."

He smiled at her. "Argus has been doing this for a long time. I would guess he's learned a few things in that time, and I would much rather learn from his experiences than my mistakes."

"I'm proud of you, son."

"Thanks, Mom," Seiko said as he returned the chess set to the study. He returned to the kitchen and hugged her. "I'll see you later. I love you."

Hannah kissed his cheek. "I love you, too. Go learn something."

Seiko smiled and left the house.

# CHAPTER 8

*You are a true knight.*

Four years later...

Seiko glanced back one more time. Satisfied that Tarik's most recent question had the teacher wholly engrossed, he dropped out the open window with barely a sound. Tarik would kill him later, but that was a problem for later. Right now, he had work to do.

He put a hand in his pocket, making sure the small silver dragon figurines were still there. His assignment today, given to him by Argus, was to sneak out of class and infiltrate three specific locations. The first was Wolf's office. The hardest part was picking the lock, but since Kolya would be out inspecting the troops at this time of day, there was little danger of someone walking by and catching him.

Seiko chose King Auren's study next. This one was a little tricky because it was on the second floor on a guard's patrol route. He waited in the bushes for the soldier to disappear around the corner then ran for the wall and began to climb.

He had reached the windowsill when he glanced down and froze. The second patrol guard was rounding the building. He held his breath, praying the man wouldn't look up, as his fingers began to cramp. Mercifully, the man moved on. Seiko climbed through the window, placing a figurine on the fireplace mantle. He left the way he'd entered, although the way down was much quicker.

He headed for the castle walls, lost in thought. This was the hard one. Watchmen were trained to notice anything out of the ordinary. As he hid in the shadow of a staircase, he noticed a commotion in the courtyard.

The horses spooked, and he noticed a young girl slip through the gate during the commotion. Intrigued, Seiko followed her. There weren't many young girls in the castle, and her dress marked her as a noble. He passed through the gate in time to see her disappear into Traitor's Grove.

Every time a noble was born, a tree was planted in the Royal Gardens. Outside the walls was a tangled copse of trees known as Traitor's Grove. Any noble that was branded a traitor had their tree removed from the Royal Gardens and transplanted to Traitor's Grove. Where the Royal Gardens were tended and manicured, Traitor's Grove was a wild tangle, rumored to be haunted.

Seiko took a deep breath and followed the girl into the grove. The trees grabbed and tore at him as if to deny him passage. Just before he began to panic, the forest released him and he found himself before a giant of a tree. The girl was collapsed at its base, sobbing.

He stared at her for a moment, eyes wide. He knew this girl! "Princess?"

She sniffed and wiped her eyes before looking at him. "Seek, what are you doing here?"

"Getting distracted by you, I guess, Princess."

She rolled her eyes. "How many times do I have to tell you to just call me Joy?"

He shook his head. "I'm sorry, but that's never going to happen and you know it."

"Then at least call me Jocelynn."

He shrugged and sat down next to her. "Are you alright?"

"I'm crying in the middle of a haunted forest," she said dryly, wiping her nose with the sleeve of her dress.

Seiko winced. "Alright, that was a dumb question. Let me try again: why are you crying?"

Jocelynn sighed and pulled her knees to her chest, wrapping her arms around them. "How about the fact that I don't matter?"

"That's ridiculous," he replied. "You're the princess. How could you not matter?"

"Because I am a princess in name only. Useless as anything but a decoy."

Seiko stared at her as the magnitude of that statement slowly sank in. He rolled to his knees, wiping tears from her face. "You are not useless. I have seen your passion. You live and love with an intensity that is so great it almost hurts me, and I know it hurts you. It's people like you who remind people like me why life is worth protecting. The last thought that would ever cross my mind when I look at you is worthless."

Jocelynn threw her arms around his neck, sobbing.

His arms tightened around her. "I don't care who told you that. You're alive and you are a beautiful princess. You matter to so many people and…you matter to me."

She released him and attempted a smile. "Thank you, Seek. I should probably get back. Mother will be worried."

He rose to his feet. "I'll walk you back."

She allowed him to pull her to her feet. "They…may not appreciate it."

"It's the right thing to do." He took her hand and led her out of Traitor's Grove.

They made it all the way to the royal wing before being spotted.

"Queen Phaedra!" a servant squealed at the sight of Jocelynn.

Phaedra came running down the hallway. She was tall and agile with thick, jet-black hair piled on top of her head. She wore a dark blue dress that ended at mid-calf, and black boots.

"Joy!" the queen cried as she fell to her knees before the children and pulled her daughter into a hug. "Where have you been? We were so worried about you."

"I'm sorry, Mother," Jocelynn mumbled against Phaedra's shoulder, crying again.

"I'm just glad you're safe."

"Seiko found me," Jocelynn said as her mother released her, eager to divert the woman's all-consuming attention.

Phaedra offered her hand to Seiko with a warm smile. "Prince Seiko, thank you for finding and returning my daughter. You are a true knight."

He bowed to her, hoping the action might cover his confusion. The sincerity in her voice surprised him. He'd never met the king or queen before but assumed, especially with Jocelynn's earlier comment, that they would be suspicious of him, as so many of their countrymen were.

"Thank you, ma'am. Your Majesty," he stammered uncertainly.

Jocelynn giggled at his uncharacteristic nervousness.

"But I'm not royalty anymore," Seiko continued, "not since my father disowned me."

Phaedra waved her hand dismissively at him, still smiling. "You will always be a prince in my book, Seiko. You should return to your house. I know Marlon has been searching for you as well."

Seiko bowed to Phaedra and Jocelynn and left.

*       *       *

When Seiko got home, he headed straight for Marlon's study.

"I see you sneaked out of your lesson and spent the day rolling in the dirt," Marlon snapped, looking pointedly at Seiko's clothes.

"Did anyone see me?" Seiko asked, matching Marlon's tone.

"No one that would have disqualified you."

"Then why are you angry?"

"Because hiding outside the castle walls is a violation of the spirit of the challenge! Hiding where no one patrols doesn't help you learn to avoid detection."

Seiko chose not to fight that observation. "The princess was crying."

"Where did you find her?"

"Clearly outside the castle walls," Seiko answered, arms folded across his chest. "Apparently, someone told her she's useless."

Marlon sighed, massaging his temples. "Kolya... She's just a child. He needs to treat her like a human being."

Seiko snorted. "If Wolf wants her to act like a princess, he needs to treat her like a princess."

Marlon looked at him sharply. "What did she tell you?"

"That she is a princess in name only, and her only use is as a decoy. Why are you smiling?"

"Because she needs someone she can trust. I'm glad she chose you."

"Who is she, and what are you trying to turn her into?"

"She is an orphan we rescued and the queen adopted. She can never rule or be given to another country in marriage. She is Kolya's apprentice, the Black Falcon to his Wolf. She is loved, unconditionally, but the reason she is here is to eventually take Kolya's place. To be Tarik's Wolf."

73

"And what is it that you expect from me?"

Marlon sighed, gesturing for Seiko to take a seat while he perched on the corner of his desk. "Kolya has a difficult time balancing love and duty, especially when it comes to Jocelynn. You need to keep her grounded and motivated when she wants to walk away because Kolya will do his best to break her. She needs someone she trusts to remind her that the pain is temporary and that her brother is going to need her."

Seiko gritted his teeth, gripping the arms of his chair. "And if I refuse to be the friend who patches her cracks only to send her back to the battlefield?"

"You would rather leave her broken?" Marlon challenged, but his voice was soft.

"I would rather she not be broken at all!" Seiko exploded, jumping up from the chair.

Marlon watched him for a moment. "Sit down, Seek, and let me tell you a story. All that pacing will get you nowhere."

Seiko growled but did as he was told.

"Once, there was a great and powerful ruler who possessed a beautiful bowl. It had been handcrafted by Malandra's master potter and given to him as a gift. It was stored in a place of honor in the treasury and only removed on special occasions, twice a year. It was taken out for New Year's and the ruler's birthday. The sight of that magnificent bowl had become the highlight of the banquet for his guests. One year, a servant retrieved the bowl, but as he carried it across the banquet hall, he tripped and the bowl crashed to the floor, shattering into pieces."

"What happened to the servant?"

"What do you think happened?"

"The destruction of what was, in effect, a national treasure." Seiko shook his head. "Did the ruler have him killed?"

Marlon smiled and continued his story. "The servant fell to his knees, begging for his life. The ruler offered him a deal: repair the bowl to his satisfaction before the end of the banquet, and he would spare the man's life. Fail, and he would become the banquet's final entertainment event.

"The servant gathered the pieces of the bowl and left the palace. He had four days to achieve an impossible task. He went to every potter in the city, trying to find someone who would agree to repair the bowl. They all refused. Any attempt to add clay to the bowl and refire it would either destroy it utterly or transform it into a hideous, disfigured thing.

"By the end of the second day, the servant was despondent, contemplating both flight and suicide. He staggered down the road whimpering, the broken bowl clutched to his chest. Someone called out to him, and he turned to see an old, hunched man. The man claimed to have a solution to the servant's problem.

"Skeptical but having no other options, he followed the man to his shop. It turned out that the old man was a goldsmith, and he was adamant that he could fix the bowl, provided the servant could acquire enough gold for the project.

"The servant sold everything he had to buy the gold he needed. The goldsmith instructed him to return on the last day of the banquet. When he returned, the goldsmith handed him a bowl-shaped object wrapped in a soft, fine cloth and told him to give it to the ruler, unopened. Trembling, the servant returned to the palace. As he entered the banquet hall, the room fell silent and all eyes turned toward him.

"He bowed before the ruler and held out the bowl, removing the cloth covering it. Everyone stared in amazement as the evening sun glittered off the gold-veined bowl. Those who had seen the bowl before it had been broken were forced to admit that it was even more magnificent now. The servant was pardoned, the bowl returned to its place of honor, and a new tradition was born."

"Tradition? Like the chalice in Wolf's office?" Seiko asked.

Marlon sighed, gaze locked on something Seiko couldn't see. *Another time,* the boy realized.

"It is an Acamarian gift meant to exemplify the strength of a bond between two parties," Marlon finally said.

"Who was it from?" Seiko knew he shouldn't push, knew from Marlon's body language that the memory was painful, but he couldn't seem to help himself.

Marlon shook his head, returning to the original topic. "Jocelynn is like that bowl, and every time Kolya challenges her, stress is applied that she was not designed to handle. These stresses will cause her to crack and even shatter if nothing is done. Gold is more malleable than fired clay and will allow her to better handle the stresses placed on her. That is your job. But before you can undertake it, you must understand that a thing is more beautiful for having been broken, and you must help her survive."

Seiko turned away, clearly struggling. "So you're saying that a person becomes more beautiful when they suffer damage and refuse to give up?"

"Yes, but it's not the suffering that makes them beautiful, it's the perseverance. Trials are tools, but when you use them to destroy hope, they become weapons. Every good thing exists because of hope," Marlon said, rising to his feet. "She is going to need someone she can trust. Kolya is injecting her with various poisons and toxins, much like I did with you, only he has isolated her, forcing her to work through it alone. I need you to be there for her. When she reaches for a hand to save her, it must be yours."

"Why?"

"Because we cannot trust another with this secret, least of all her brother." Marlon smiled, placing a hand on Seiko's shoulder. "I would not ask this of you if I did not think you capable. Get some rest, my son. I'll see you in the morning."

Seiko wrapped his arms around Marlon and pressed his face into his chest. There was more going on than he understood. "I won't let you down."

Marlon tousled his hair, smiling. "You never have."

*   *   *

Tarik glared at Seiko, arms folded across his chest. "I hope you enjoyed yourself yesterday."

"As a matter of fact, I did," Seiko said with a grin. "Did you learn something?"

"Yeah," Tarik snapped, taking a step toward him, hands balled into fists. "I learned that my hand cramps and I get a headache when I have to list and describe every noble house's standard from memory all by myself because you decided to skip class!"

"He was really mad, then."

"You think?"

"I swiped you a peace offering," Seiko said, producing three cookies.

"You can't buy your way…are those gingerbread?" Tarik asked.

Seiko laughed. "They're fresh." There was a yell from the kitchen, and Seiko grabbed Tarik's arm. "Really fresh. Run!"

*   *   *

They finished their cookies on the castle wall, out of sight of the kitchen staff.

"Now what?" Tarik asked.

77

"How about hide-and-seek?"

"No fun with only two people."

"What about your sister? She's small. I bet she'd be good at it."

"That's…actually a good point. I'll go see if she's free. Meet me in the garden."

Seiko grinned as Tarik walked away.

*          *          *

Jocelynn, Tarik, and Seiko spent the whole day playing hide-and-seek and stealing pastries from the kitchens. At the end of the day, the three of them were lying in the grass, looking up at the clouds.

"Thanks, Riki," Jocelynn said with a smile. "I had fun today."

"Hey, we're going for a ride tomorrow. You should come with us," Seiko said, propping himself up on his elbow.

"Princess Jocelynn!" a servant called. "Your mother requests your presence in her room."

Jocelynn rolled her eyes. "A ride sounds like fun! Unfortunately, I have to get ready for supper, but I'll see you tomorrow, and thanks again."

# CHAPTER 9

*He always sends you.*

Seiko woke up and got dressed quickly, excited for the day. When he entered the dining room, he paused. Hannah and Marlon stood with Marlon's travel bag on the counter between them. "You're leaving?" Seiko asked as his heart sank.

Marlon turned to look at him. "I have to. Zefros claims that Ijlal is pillaging its border towns."

"That doesn't have anything to do with us."

"They petitioned King Auren to provide a neutral party to mediate the dispute. He agreed and chose to send me."

Seiko rolled his eyes, arms folded across his chest. "He always sends you."

"Yes, he does," Marlon agreed. "Can you suggest a better person to deal with delicate diplomatic matters, especially in regard to Ryu and Ijlal?"

Seiko looked at the floor, body rigid.

"So that's what this is about." Marlon dropped to one knee so he was at eye level with Seiko. "It's not my absence that's bothering you. It's my proximity to your father."

Seiko looked up, hands clenched by his sides. "You're tempting fate, Argus. My father wants you dead, and not in the abstract 'it would make my life easier if he were dead' kind of way. He wants to rip your head from your shoulders and mount it over his fireplace, and that was before you saved me."

"Seek, I have to go," Marlon said slowly.

"Do you really think he's raiding those villages?"

"I wouldn't put it past him, but he's shrewd enough that there won't be any evidence that I can trace back to him. If I side with Ryu, I fear the attacks will only increase in frequency as he continues to test us. However, if I side with Zefros and demand concessions without proof, I appear biased—only concerned with punishing a country I have a vendetta against."

"Which means you'll have to come up with a compromise."

"More specifically, a compromise everyone hates more or less equally."

"I hate politics," Seiko muttered.

Marlon ruffled his hair as he rose. "So do I. Unfortunately, it is necessary. I will be fine, Seek. Your father cannot harm me without starting a war, and he's not prepared for that yet."

Seiko hugged him. "Stay safe, and I'll see you when you return."

Marlon returned his hug. "Take care of your mother for me."

"Always," Seiko said as Marlon kissed Hannah and left.

"He'll be alright. He always is," Hannah said as Seiko bit his lip.

"One slip is all it takes."

"We are not as fragile as you believe, my son."

"All humans are fragile," Seiko said shortly. Then, as if realizing what he'd said, he bowed to her. "I apologize, Mother. I'm just worried for him. You are correct."

"Of course I am," she said, hands on her hips. "Now, aren't you supposed to go riding with the prince this morning?"

"Oh, right." He kissed her cheek and headed out the door.

*　　　　　*　　　　　*

Seiko entered the courtyard and slowed when he saw Tarik with only two horses. "Where's your sister?"

"She's not feeling well," Tarik answered. "Mother said to go without her."

"She was fine yesterday."

Tarik shrugged. "Mother says she has a weak constitution. She'll be fine in a day or so. Come on."

Seiko mounted his horse and followed Tarik but couldn't help glancing up at Jocelynn's bedroom window, suspicious.

*　　　　　*　　　　　*

Tarik and Seiko dismounted in the courtyard. Seiko once again found himself looking up at Jocelynn's bedroom window.

"Forget about her. She'll be fine," Tarik laughed playfully, punching Seiko's shoulder. "This happens all the time."

"Alright, alright," Seiko muttered, shrugging him off.

As they began weapons practice, Seiko tried to focus on his opponent but couldn't stop worrying about Jocelynn. He didn't believe for a moment that she'd just happened to get sick two days after he talked her off a ledge, but the idea that Kolya would poison her again so soon after her breakdown…

"Seiko!" Kolya snapped, bringing Seiko's focus back to his opponent just in time to duck. The wooden sword sailed through the air where his head had been seconds before.

Seiko straightened, eyes downcast, as Kolya towered over him, glaring. "Your head's not here, boy. You are putting yourself and everyone here in danger. Find a way to focus or remove yourself from this facility. Am I clear?"

Seiko glared up at Kolya then quickly away, hands clenched by his sides. He wanted to shout at Kolya, to demand to know what he had done to Jocelynn. Instead, he took a deep breath, shifted his grip on his sword, and bowed stiffly. "Yes, Wolf."

"And if I have to remind you again, I will throw you out myself."

Seiko sighed and turned back to his partner.

*      *      *

"What was that about?" Tarik asked, catching up to Seiko after practice. "I mean, sure, you were distracted, but he was way harsher with you than he usually is even with students that show up hungover. Besides, even distracted, you're still better than most of that class."

*Because it's not just Jocelynn he's testing,* Seiko realized. *With Argus gone, he's testing me as well. How far is he willing to push her just to see my reaction?* He glanced at Tarik and shrugged. "It's his class, he makes the rules. I guess he saw something you didn't."

"Or maybe he's having a bad day and decided to take it out on you."

Seiko didn't respond.

*      *      *

Seiko entered the house that night and collapsed into the chair at the dining room table.

"What's wrong, son?" Hannah asked as they began to eat.

He hesitated. "I don't know for sure that anything is wrong."

"Your intuition is rarely misleading," she observed. "What happened?"

"It's Jocelynn, the princess," Seiko blurted. "She was supposed to go riding with Tarik and me this morning, but Tarik said she wasn't feeling well. She was fine yesterday, and no one else is sick."

"And what do you think is going on?"

Seiko growled in frustration. "I think Wolf poisoned her again, as Argus did with me, to desensitize her to certain toxins. I just can't fathom why he would do this to her two days after she was ready to give up. Poisoning is as much a psychological trial as it is a physiological one. The body tends to give up when the mind does, and Wolf knows it."

"If you're right," Hannah said slowly, "what she needs right now is a friend to remind her what's real and what's not. That's what Marlon intended you to be."

Seiko looked down at his plate, frustrated. "How? I'm not supposed to be in the royal wing of the castle, much less the princess's room after dark."

"According to Marlon, it's only illegal if they catch you. A rule is only as strong as your ability to enforce it."

*       *       *

Seiko sneaked out of the house later that night. He avoided the guards, moving from shadow to shadow. When he reached the base of the castle, he quickly located Jocelynn's window and began to climb.

It was a longer climb than he had anticipated, and he'd never attempted something like this in the dark. He gritted his teeth and kept climbing. By the time he reached her window, his arms were shaking from exertion. He tapped softly on the glass. He heard a moan but no movement, and he realized with a start that he had no backup plan if Jocelynn didn't open the window. He would never survive the climb back down without a chance to rest. Heart hammering, he knocked again as loudly as he dared.

"Seek, what are you doing?" Jocelynn mumbled as she opened the window.

He scrambled into the room, catching her before she could fall out the window and helping her sit down on her bed.

"You're not sick," he said, watching her.

She pulled her blanket tightly around her shoulders. "Cocktail toxin and a hallucinogen. Should be almost over."

Seiko shook his head and sat beside her. He didn't know how, but Kolya and Marlon had developed a time-release second dose designed to hit you just as you started to relax.

Jocelynn leaned against him as the second dose rocked her, and her eyes began to dart wildly. She buried her face in his shoulder with a strangled cry. Seiko began to rock her, humming softly and rubbing soothing circles on her back. At last her sobs subsided, and exhaustion claimed her.

He checked her pulse and respiration rate. Satisfied that they were normalizing, he turned his attention to the injection site. It was a sickly greenish-purple color, but it appeared to be fading. Realizing that she was truly sleeping and unlikely to have another episode, he laid her on her bed and carefully spread the blanket over her. Not wanting her to think he had just been part of the hallucination, he moved to her desk and wrote her a letter.

*Jocelynn,*

*I know what they're doing to you and why because it's been done to me. I know how it feels to be lost and alone, trapped in the nightmares of your mind, and I know you have no one to talk to. They expect you to be solitary and strong because that's what they need from the Black Falcon, but all of them, especially Wolf, forget that you are still a child and sometimes you just need to scream. Traitor's Grove is a good place to go. The adults won't search for you there, and if you need to talk, wait by the giant tree where I found you. I'll always come for you.*

*My heart is forever yours, Princess.*

*Seiko Kasun*

*        *        *

Marlon returned a week later and, despite his exhaustion, headed straight for his office.

"How was your trip?" Kolya asked, already there waiting for him.

Marlon glared at him as he collapsed into the chair behind his desk. "I survived, clearly."

Kolya rolled his eyes.

"Zefros is increasing the frequency and number of patrols on their northern border," Marlon reported, "and Ijlal has agreed to hunt down the bandits seeking refuge on their lands and deliver them to Zefros for punishment."

"So Ryu gets to handpick his scapegoats and we're still headed for war, just not tomorrow."

Marlon rubbed his temples, groaning. "With Ryu ruling a country, we're always headed for war. The only question is: how long can we delay him?"

Kolya grunted, pushing himself away from the wall. "You look like crap. This stuff can wait. Go home. Your wife and son are worried about you."

Marlon hesitated, glancing at the stack of reports on his desk.

"No, go home," Kolya growled, pulling him to his feet. "Go see your family then get to bed. Everything here can wait. I checked."

Marlon raised an eyebrow. "So you looked at it, you just didn't bother to do any of it."

Kolya grinned. "Why would I ever actually do your work?"

Marlon laughed and headed for the door.

"And Raven?" Kolya called. "It's good to have you back."

# CHAPTER 10



*What do you expect of me?*


T*hree years later…*

Marlon awoke to the smell of baking. He got dressed and entered the kitchen to find Hannah already up and working. She smiled at him and gestured to the letter on the counter with her floured hands.

He picked it up. It was sealed with a small oak leaf frozen and amber. "Is Seek still asleep?"

She laughed. "Your son, sleep past sunrise?"

He smiled and broke the seal on the letter.


*Argus, there is an urgent matter we need to discuss.*
*Aysel*


"Is something wrong?" Hannah asked, watching his face.

Marlon looked at her and shrugged. "Who knows? Aderes and her sirens never were big on details, but they don't send letters without cause."

Hannah leaned across the counter and kissed him. "Go see what world-altering crisis is imminent that only you can solve."

He smiled and pocketed the letter. "I'll see you tonight."
She sighed as he walked out the door.

*        *        *

Marlon entered Aderes' forest, on edge as a path opened before him. Aderes controlled the forest, so the path appearing certainly wasn't abnormal, but leading him into the forest meant she didn't want to be overheard.

The path opened onto a clearing where a woman was waiting for him.

"Aderes?" he asked.

She cocked her head. "Hello, Raven, you sound surprised. Am I not allowed to appear when and where I please in my domain?"

"Of course. I would never dream of questioning your sovereignty," Marlon stammered with a bow. "But the letter I received was from Aysel. I expected to be meeting her."

Aderes shrugged. "My daughter is not currently within my domain. This threat is such that she has already left to combat it."

"Well, that's ominous. I can't remember the last time you sent her to deal with a threat in person. What can you tell me?"

"There is a previously unknown dragon terrorizing the forest in the northern reaches of your imaginary kingdom."

"Sedria is very much a real entity, and worth defending."

Aderes shrugged. "Lines on a piece of parchment that are only true so long as everyone agrees on them. The land acknowledges no ruler save those who affect her change."

"So what's this about a dragon terrorizing the trees?"

"I'm certain he is attacking villages in the area as well, but as you know, I received my information from the trees, and he is burning them."

"You sent Aysel to confront him. Isn't she afraid of dragons?"

"Aysel is a siren, the last of my true daughters. She fears nothing. Not even death. What she has is a realistic understanding and respect for a dragon's power as well as obstinate distrust in a group that has proven their selfishness and utter disregard for life with every incarnation."

"What do you expect of me?"

Aderes smiled. "No more than what I always expect: observe and find a way to neutralize the threat to your people. You've faced dragons before."

"Driven them off, yes, but not killed. If this one's already staked his claim, we'll have to find a way."

"You always do," Aderes said with a warm smile. "You don't believe in impossibilities."

"We'll head out tomorrow."

"And Raven?" she called as he turned to go. "Take your son with you. His assistance could prove invaluable."

Marlon left, troubled.

*       *       *

Later that night, Marlon was eating supper with his family, clearly distracted.

"Do you want to talk about it?" Hannah asked, setting her fork down.

"What?" Marlon asked, realizing he had only eaten about three bites of his food.

Hannah glanced at Seiko and then back at her husband. "You met with her. What did she want?"

"Who?" Seiko asked curiously.

"Aderes," Marlon answered.

Seiko studied his face. "The woman who saved my life?"

"Yes. She's…well, not a friend, exactly, but an ally and a reliable source of information."

"Her daughter, Aysel, helps refugees reach me safely," Hannah added.

"What did she say?" Seiko asked.

Marlon sighed. "She told me there's a dragon carving a path of destruction along our northern border."

Seiko pushed food around on his plate, suddenly not hungry. "I've seen no reports indicating an actual dragon in that region. Where did she get her information?"

Marlon laughed. "She almost always gets her information before we do. She claims most of it comes from the trees."

"And you believe her?"

"Always," Marlon said with a gentle smile. "She brought me you, didn't she?"

Seiko thought about this for a moment. Finally, he looked at Marlon. "Do you trust her?"

Marlon pursed his lips and sat back, considering the question. "Not blindly," he answered. "She is not an enemy and has never been duplicitous, but neither does she have any particular loyalty to Sedria or any country. She calls them imagined ideals that mean less than nothing to the natural world. I am cognizant of the fact that any information she chooses to share with us also benefits her in some way. To answer your question, I believe her when she speaks, but I never trust her to give me the whole story."

"Then what will you do?"

"Not I, we," Marlon corrected with a smile. "*We* are leaving in the morning to gauge and neutralize this threat."

Seiko's eyes widened. "You want me to come with you?"

"You are immune to dragonsbane and resistant to dragon fire.

You could be a great asset in this fight."

"Thank you, Argus," Seiko said, pushing himself to his feet, supper forgotten. "I won't disappoint you."

"You never have," Marlon answered with a smile.

Hannah took Marlon's hand as Seiko rushed from the room. Marlon looked at her worried expression and squeezed her hand.

"You're taking our son to fight a dragon," she stated.

"Darling, he needs to do what he was born for," he said softly.

"This will make him a target. If his father learns he can slay his kind…"

"He's already a target. Everyone in this house is a target. I can't protect him forever."

Hannah gritted her teeth, her grip on his hand tightening. "Just make sure he has the skills to survive."

"Of course. I'm his mentor, that's my job."

"You are his father, which makes his continued survival not just your job but your responsibility."

Marlon winced, rubbing circles on her hand with his thumb. "I know, but if Aderes suggested sending him, he's ready. For whatever reason, he's as important to her plans as he is to us."

"I'm not sure if that comforts me or makes me more worried," she sighed.

He chuckled and kissed her cheek. "I had the same thought."

# CHAPTER 11

*Na'ain threla, the call of the void.*

Seiko and Marlon met Aysel in a tavern in the small village of Avery.

"I see you brought your dragon," she said as she sat down, nose wrinkled in disgust.

"At your mother's insistence," Marlon said gently. "What have you seen?"

Aysel sniffed, turning away from Seiko. "There's definitely a dragon up here destroying everything it can find."

Marlon slid a drink over to her. "What type? We've still had no verifiable reports of a dragon near the city."

"I didn't stop to ask his name while he was trying to burn down the forest that I was protecting." She shrugged. "I would guess he's in his mid-twenties, though."

"You protected the forest but let him burn villages?" Seiko asked.

"Yes. I chose the forest," she snapped, glaring at him. "Trees don't move fast enough to get away from dragon fire. People at least have a chance on their own."

"Why do you think he's in his twenties?" Marlon asked, drawing

Aysel's attention away from Seiko.

She shrugged. "An older dragon would have known how to get around my protection spell. He just beat his head against it until he gave up. Also, dragons older than about thirty-two tend to stay in human form. The urge to return to the stars is generally too strong to resist after that age."

Seiko cocked his head, trying to line up this new information with what he knew of his father and brother. He'd changed forms, and he'd seen Kana change many times to hunt or just for fun. He realized he could count the number of times he'd seen or heard of Ryu transforming on one hand, and they had become less frequent as he'd gotten older.

"The stars have a term for it. They call it *na'ain threla*. The call of the void. Dragons are born of the void, and over time, the call becomes harder to ignore," Aysel explained. "Most try to stave off this compulsion as long as possible, as they cannot survive the transition through the atmosphere. Their blood combusts in their bodies and they burn up from the inside out. The stars use these new raw materials to create another dragon, and the cycle is perpetuated."

Seiko looked at her. "I had wondered why my father so rarely takes his true form."

"So about this dragon…" Marlon said, bringing them back to the task at hand. "Where do you think he's headed?"

"He's following the coast. I think he's decided the forests aren't worth his time."

"And you're sure it's not a blood dragon?"

Aysel smiled indulgently at him. "I'm sure."

"What's a blood dragon?" Seiko asked, looking from one to the other.

"Blood dragons are a larger, more aggressive type of dragon

that feeds on despair," Aysel answered. "And they are all female."

Seiko stared at her, eyes wide. That just left him with so many more questions!

"And not what we're here for," Marlon said. "Thank you for your help, Aysel."

She smiled at him and rose. "Anything for you, Argus. Good luck."

"Thank you for your help," Seiko added.

Aysel wrinkled her nose before she turned and left the tavern.

"She doesn't like me."

Marlon sighed. "It's not personal, Seek. Her sisters were all killed or corrupted by the dragons. She has a hard time believing that a dragon may exist that is not everything she was created to stand against."

"Can't really blame her," Seiko said. "My own experience has proven her mistrust is well placed."

Marlon rose, and Seiko followed suit. "We need to find that dragon before he attacks again."

*   *   *

"Are we actually going to fight this dragon?" Seiko asked, looking around the campfire. "Just us?"

Marlon cocked his head. "What would you do if a group of marauders were plundering our villages?"

The boy stuck his tongue between his teeth as he brushed dragonsbane on a spear point. "I would stop them by whatever means necessary. I guess I asked the wrong question. My father claims that no mortal can slay a dragon, and even King Auren didn't challenge that assertion during the war. The war ended because you threatened his horde, not his person, which makes my question:

How do you intend to kill this dragon, I suppose."

Marlon took half the arrows Seiko had coated in dragonsbane and placed them in his quiver. "Everything dies. The trick is knowing how and why. Dragons have very tough, scaly hides, and their blood combusts when it comes in contact with the air. This makes killing them difficult but not impossible. Dragonsbane is a compound that allows ordinary blades to penetrate a dragon's hide. The general strategy when fighting a dragon is to rip through its wings to ground it, and then do enough damage that he bleeds out or you get lucky and hit a vital organ."

"This sounds like an expensive fight both in terms of equipment and lives."

"It is. That's the main reason King Auren offered Ryu the terms he did after the last war. We avoid fighting dragons when we can, but dragons generally don't negotiate and won't stop unless they are forced to. When they become a threat, they must be killed as quickly as possible."

Seiko finished applying dragonsbane to the soldiers' weapons in silence.

＊ ＊ ＊

They had been riding for hours with no sign of the dragon they were supposed to be hunting.

Seiko was nodding off in his saddle. He hadn't slept well the night before, and the rolling gate of his horse had lulled him into a state of drowsiness.

"Get down!" Marlon yelled, leaping off his horse.

"What?" Seiko asked as his head came up. His horse screamed and reared, dumping him onto the ground.

Marlon grabbed him by the arm and dragged him out of the

way as the dragon dove, breathing fire.

Seiko grimaced in pain and scrambled to his feet as Marlon released him. He stared as the dragon banked for another pass. It was bigger than he had expected, but then he'd only had Kana's dragon for reference.

It was dark brown and moved almost like it was turning in slow motion.

"We need to ground him!" Marlon shouted.

The horses had initially panicked, but they were battle-trained and now huddled a little ways away just inside the shelter of a copse of trees. The soldiers retrieved their weapons and returned to Marlon as the dragon dove again.

"Aim for the wings," Marlon said, waiting until the dragon snapped its wings open to level out its flight before calling out the order to "Fire!"

They let fly, but only a few projectiles managed to penetrate the leathery skin of the dragon's wings. He faltered for a moment, more from surprise and pain than any inability to remain airborne.

The men dove out of the way as the dragon breathed a line of fire at them and began circling again. One man didn't dodge in time and screamed as he was engulfed in flames.

Seiko retched as the smell of sulfur and burning flesh filled the air.

Marlon gritted his teeth. "Reload! He's coming around again!"

"It's going to take forever to ground him like this," Seiko said.

"Into the trees!" a voice called. "Force him to land."

"Aysel?" Marlon asked. "I thought you weren't helping."

"Just do it," she snapped, appearing at the tree line.

"Fall back into the forest, weapons ready!" Marlon roared.

The dragon landed heavily as the men ran into the trees, growling in frustration. Before he could fold his wings against his body, a thick tree branch suddenly grew out of the copse of trees and punched a hole in his left wing. He screamed and thrashed as the branch curved around his back and punctured his other wing.

Panicked, the dragon launched himself into the air. He succeeded in breaking the branch but shredded his wings in the process. Both Aysel and the dragon screamed, and there was a loud crash from deeper in the copse of trees.

"Now!" Marlon yelled, running at the dragon and brandishing a spear. Seiko and the soldiers followed him.

The dragon roared as they spread out, flanking him. He had managed to fold one damaged wing against his body, but the other dragged on the ground, broken and useless. He shifted his attention from one group of men to the other, but every time he did, they would dart in and stab him.

The men had to be careful to avoid the dragon's blood as it ran down his body and combusted. As the dragon's gaze shifted, Marlon ducked under the broken wing and shoved his spear into his armpit, deep into his rib cage.

The dragon screamed and smacked Marlon with his foreleg. He flew through the air and landed on his back, air driven from his lungs.

"Argus!" Seiko cried. He took a step toward him and then realized the spear was still lodged in the dragon's side. Blood was beginning to ooze out and combust, but the spear was plugging the hole.

Seiko took a deep breath and darted under the dragon's wing, reaching for the spear. He grabbed it and pulled but it didn't budge, stuck on something inside the beast. He set his feet and twisted the haft of the spear viciously.

The dragon screamed and thrashed. Seiko grunted as the dragon's foreleg hit him and he flew through the air. His flight was cut short when he struck its damaged wing and landed on a heap on the ground, Marlon's spear clutched in a white-knuckle grip.

The dragon roared and staggered sideways as blood and fire gushed from the wound. Seiko yelped and rolled away, dropping the spear as his arm caught fire. Marlon ran to him as the dragon's thrashing slowed.

"Don't touch me!" Seiko cried as he turned toward Marlon, holding his injured arm away.

Marlon slid to a stop, eyes fixed on Seiko's arm. It was covered in a clear, silver, viscous fluid.

Aysel crouched before Seiko as he fell to his knees with a hiss. "Don't touch me," Seiko said as she reached for his arm.

She shook her head, silk growing out of her fingertips, wrapping around his arm in a cocoon. "Jericho won't harm me."

Seiko stared as the cocoon fell away to reveal new skin covering his arm.

"You will still be sore, but you're not a danger to others, and my debt is repaid," Aysel said as she rose and faded into the trees.

Marlon smiled and helped Seiko to his feet. "Congratulations. You just killed your first dragon."

Shaking his head, Seiko looked at the carnage around them. "This was a group effort."

*       *       *

Weeks later, Seiko was out in the practice yard sparring with Tarik. They were both breathing hard and sweating.

Seiko lunged at an opening in Tarik's defense but the prince had anticipated this. He blocked with his shield and countered, rapping Seiko on the arm with his wooden practice sword.

Seiko winced as he backpedaled, shaking his arm to get rid of the stinging sensation. "You're getting better," he said grudgingly.

Tarik grinned, trying to catch his breath.

"Panther Seiko Kasun!" someone called out. The boys turned toward the fence, seeing a page waving to them. "Raven requests your presence in his office."

Seiko sighed. "I'm coming."

"He said at your convenience."

Seiko laughed. "We're at a good stopping point, and you don't keep the Raven of Sedria waiting, even if you do live in his house."

Tarik raised his arm in a gesture of parting. "I'll see you later, dragon slayer."

Seiko rolled his eyes as he returned his weapons to the barrel and headed for the castle. Despite his cavalier attitude, he was nervous. Raven rarely called him to his office, and never this publicly. Word that he'd been the one to kill the dragon had quickly spread, and many had taken to calling him dragon slayer. He wondered if this meeting had anything to do with that. He took a deep breath and knocked on Marlon's office door.

"Come in," Marlon called.

Seiko entered and stood before Marlon's desk, hands clasped behind his back. "You asked to see me, Raven?"

Marlon gave him a reassuring smile. "Sit down. How are you feeling?"

Seiko sat in the chair, looking at his arm. "I'm fine. No permanent damage, if that's what you're asking." He grimaced as he rotated his arm. "Still a little slow, and Tarik's gotten better with his counter."

Marlon's lips quirked. "Aderes was correct. You do have some innate resistance to dragon fire."

Seiko cocked his head. "Is that significant?"

"It could be, especially if we have to deal with dragon incursions on a more regular basis. Based on your training and your performance on your last mission, I'm promoting you to Shark effective immediately and assigning you your own squad."

Seiko furrowed his brow.

"Is there something wrong?"

"It's just…I'm only sixteen, and your son. Are you sure that's wise?"

Marlon smiled. "Auren suggested the promotion, and Kolya agreed."

Seiko snorted. "Wolf doesn't even like me."

"You've impressed a lot of people. Your duties and classes have not changed, but if Aysel hadn't helped us in that last battle, a lot more soldiers would be dead. You and your squad will be charged with finding a reliable way to take these monsters down without relying on magic or luck."

"Very well, Raven."

"Dismissed."

Seiko saluted and left the office.

*    *    *

Seiko looked up as Tarik dropped into the chair beside him. "What's your problem?"

"The ball tonight," Tarik groaned.

Seiko laughed. "You are a prince. Balls tend to happen periodically."

Tarik rolled his eyes. "Yeah, I know, but Mom's letting Joy come."

Seiko was not quite able to keep the grin off his face. "She's about that age."

"She's a child!"

"She's thirteen," Seiko corrected softly. "She has to start growing up sometime."

Tarik glared at him and they finished their lunch in awkward silence.

*　　　　　*　　　　　*

Seiko returned to his house to get ready for the ball. He and Hannah always got ready together as Marlon was busy with security and final checks in the castle.

Hannah had chosen to wear a soft blue silk dress with tight sleeves and sapphire jewelry. "Have you spoken with Princess Jocelynn today?" she asked, looking at him in the mirror.

Seiko shook his head as he finished buttoning the back of her dress. "No. Why?"

She shrugged. "I just remember how nervous you were before your first ball. There are a lot of expectations on her, and she seems to take everything so seriously."

He stepped away from her, and she turned to survey his outfit. He was wearing a navy-blue outfit with silver sharks embroidered onto the sleeves of his jacket. "I suspect she has spent the day with Queen Phaedra getting ready. This whole thing has Tarik pretty irritated, though."

Hannah straightened his shirt and buttoned his cuffs. "What do you mean?"

"He thinks his sister's too young to be attending, but she's older than we were when we started attending official functions. I don't get why he's so upset about this."

She pursed her lips. "Well, no boy likes to acknowledge his sister's growing up."

"It feels like it's more than that."

Hannah shrugged. "You know him better than most. Is he protective or controlling?"

"Maybe both," he answered, brow knit.

She smiled and kissed his cheek. "Your girl walks a dangerous path. Watch out for her."

*    *    *

Seiko looked up as Tarik and Jocelynn entered the ballroom. Tarik was dressed in dark purple and silver with a silver circlet on his head. He wore polished black boots with his pants tucked into them. Dressed in much lighter hues, Jocelynn fairly shone as Tarik helped her navigate the staircase into the ballroom. She wore a floor-length hoop skirt with a scoop-neck corset top and full sleeves. She wore a sparkling, diamond-studded tiara and matching necklace. Clearly, her mother intended for her to be the center of attention.

Watching her dance with her brother, he found it hard to believe she was only thirteen. Once the dance was over, Jocelynn's attention was claimed by a string of young noblemen. He watched as her posture tensed after every dance, scanning the crowd until she found her target: Tarik.

Finally, Seiko set his drink down and approached her, placing a gentle hand on her shoulder. She spun quickly to face him.

"Easy," he said with a smile as he kissed her hand. "You're supposed to be enjoying yourself, remember? May I have this dance?"

Jocelynn smiled and dropped into a curtsy. "Of course."

Seiko spun her around as the music began, smiling as she visibly relaxed in his arms. "How many daggers did you manage to sneak under that dress?" he whispered in her ear.

She laughed as he spun her around. "I had five. Kolya found

three, took two, and completely missed my blowgun."

"That's my girl," Seiko said with a smile as the song ended.

He glanced across the ballroom and sighed. She looked over her shoulder to see Tarik headed toward them, nostrils flaring.

"It appears I should take my leave and flirt with some of the other pretty ladies in attendance," Seiko said.

"Oh, so I'm just one of many?" she teased.

Seiko glanced at Tarik and then back at Jocelynn. He smiled and moved so that his lips brushed her ear when he spoke. "You are the most beautiful princess. No one in this room, or this world, can hold a candle to you." He kissed her hand and strode away just before Tarik reached them.

*  *  *

Late evening found Seiko up in the castle's rooftop arcade. It was a covered walkway at the top of the castle that connected the east and west towers, and it was the closest he could get to the dark open sky within the city. With the torches and the crowds muted and below him, it was one of the few places he felt at peace. Traitor's Grove was Jocelynn's place, but this…this was his refuge, away from the stifling light and noise below him, in the silence and starlight.

"Oh, my son, you wear your heart on your sleeve," a voice said from somewhere above him.

A puzzled expression crossed Seiko's face. "So it wasn't just a one-time deal. Who are you?"

The voice chuckled. "Last time you listened to my advice, it saved your life. You would distrust me now?"

Seiko folded his arms across his chest. "There are very few people I truly trust, and you haven't spoken to me in six years. I don't know who you are, and I've never seen your face. Why should I trust you?"

"Seeing my face is not a request I could grant even if I were so inclined, and if I told you who I was, you wouldn't believe me. You should trust me because I'm the reason you exist, and I've already saved your life once."

Seiko leaned against a pillar. "Let's say I believe you. What do you want?"

"You were gifted with a silver tongue. Already, you've begun to make women young and old swoon over you."

Seiko shrugged, eyes closed.

"You must be careful, for your attention has already been claimed, and soon your heart will be, as well."

Seiko's eyes snapped open and he straightened off the column. "She is a child, and I would not take advantage of her trust."

"She will not be a child forever, and her brother has already realized this. Three years is not such a great span of time, and it will grow shorter with the living. Watch what you say, but more than anything, watch over her. She believes her worth is measured by her ability to protect her charge, and she will die for that cause because to do otherwise would be to prove her worthlessness."

"That's a lie!" Seiko growled, hands clenched into fists. "You don't know her like I do. She knows her value."

"Only sometimes," the voice said as it faded. "And not when it matters."

"She's not your tool," Seiko said. "And neither am I."

# CHAPTER 12

*You're going to have your work cut out for you.*

**M**onths later...

"Raven, you wanted to see me?" Seiko asked, knocking on Marlon's open door.

"Yes. Come in," Marlon said with a smile. "And shut the door."

Seiko obeyed, studying the other man in the room with Marlon. He was taller than Seiko by a good four inches and looked to be in his mid-twenties. He had thick black hair and an easygoing smile that was at odds with his intimidating appearance.

"Seek, this is Trevor," Marlon said, watching them size each other up. "He'll be your adjutant."

"Badger," Seiko said, glancing at the insignia embossed on Trevor's shoulder.

Trevor clasped Seiko's hand in a firm, strong grip. "Shark."

"You pulled the squad together already?" Seiko asked, curious.

Marlon sat back with a smile. "I do have some practice, son. Your squad consists of eight plus the two of you. They will meet you tomorrow after morning drills. I've already briefed Trevor. I'll let him fill you in."

"How about we go for a ride?" Seiko suggested.

Trevor smiled. "Horses are saddled by the gate."

*     *     *

"Tell me about yourself, Trevor," Seiko said once they were out of sight of the castle.

Trevor shrugged. "There's not much to tell. I was promoted recently, my parents are dead, and I have very few friends."

"What made you volunteer to join a squad whose express purpose is to hunt dragons?"

"I'm Ijlala," he said quietly.

Seiko pulled his horse to a stop and stared at Trevor.

"I've seen the kind of damage dragons can do if left unchecked," Trevor said.

"I wouldn't have guessed. Are we going to have a problem?"

"Because you're a dragon, or because you're Ryu's son?" Trevor asked, meeting his gaze.

"Both," Seiko decided.

"I've seen how you deal with your problems, and Raven put you in charge of this squad. He didn't get to be where he is by misjudging people. I will have no issues following your orders, Shark."

Seiko took a deep breath, refocusing on the purpose of their ride as they started moving again. "Tell me about the squad."

"Well, like Raven said, there are eight of them: Nicholas, Aaron, Thomas, Cameron, Joseph, Logan, Ethan, and Dylan. Cam and Ronnie are sharpshooters. Tom and Logan are better at mid-range, throwing axes and daggers, mostly. Nick and Dylan are the heavy hitters, but please don't ask them to throw anything, ever. They can be trusted with a crossbow, if necessary. Joe and Ethan are jacks."

"Jacks?" Seiko repeated.

"Jack-of-all-trades, master of none," Trevor answered. "They're good at pretty much anything and should easily adapt to any situation."

"Sounds like a well-rounded group."

"Raven's been working on this squad for some time now, or so I hear, but you're going to have your work cut out for you."

"What does that mean?"

Trevor sighed. "I know most of these men from previous assignments, and I believe they volunteered for this squad for one of two reasons. They either want the pay increase or think introducing themselves as a dragon slayer is a good way to impress women. But there's more to it, isn't there? Killing a dragon is going to be a lot more difficult than they think."

Seiko gritted his teeth, hands tightening on his reins. "Dragons are the size of barns, with scales as tough as plate armor, and they don't fight at close range if they can help it. The weakest part of a dragon is its wings, but I use that term loosely. Trying to puncture a dragon's wing is like trying to punch a hole in thick-cured leather with a stick."

"What about that stuff that can eat through a dragon's hide?"

"Dragonsbane," Seiko said. "It's useful, but the reaction isn't instantaneous. A weapon coated in dragonsbane must be embedded in the dragon or caught between its scales for the compound to have enough time to be effective."

Trevor whistled softly. "What's the strategy for fighting a beast like that?"

"The current strategy is to pepper the dragon with arrows and hope enough of them stick that the dragonsbane can perforate at least one of the dragon's wings and cause it to crash. Once it's grounded, we move in with spears and heavy melee weapons and attempt to puncture vital organs while avoiding its breath, claws, teeth, tail, and combusting blood."

"Every dragon we take down is going to cost lives."

"But how many are we saving in the process?"

"I know, I know," Trevor said. "But if these men really understood that, at least half of them wouldn't have volunteered."

"That's true of all wars," Seiko said softly.

They rode back to the castle in silence.

# CHAPTER 13

*The only true test is the enemy.*

Seiko shook his head as he leaned against the railing watching Trevor run drills with the squad. It had been almost a year, and they had done little more than escort caravans and track bandits.

"Logan!" Trevor yelled, his voice ringing out across the arena.

Logan yelped and dropped his wooden practice sword as Cameron's sword hit him in the arm. "Trev, my head hurts and I can't concentrate with all this light!" he whined.

"It's not my fault you were out late last night again. I warned you carousing would have consequences," Trevor answered, picking up his sword and tossing it to him, which he missed.

Logan cried out as it smacked him in the face. Cameron winced.

"How are they doing?" Marlon asked, leaning against the railing beside Seiko.

Seiko shrugged. "Aside from the immaturity and occasional pigheadedness, as well as can be expected. Some of them don't think they'll ever see a dragon. They're starting to think they've been played."

"Well, they're about to be wrong."

Seiko blinked and turned to look at him. "What?"

Trevor and Cameron stopped what they were doing, noticing Seiko's posture stiffen. The others followed suit.

"Oslian sailors have sighted a blood dragon near the Isle of Pation. It's setting fire to their whaling vessels and raiding their villages."

"I get that it's a dragon," Seiko said, "but politically speaking, how is this our concern?"

Marlon glanced over Seiko's shoulder at the soldiers trying to casually eavesdrop on their conversation.

Realizing they had been caught, Trevor turned to the squad and yelled, "All of you, down to the lake, swim ten laps, then run back to the barracks! Anyone who beats Cam gets an extra hour of sleep!"

They all groaned.

"Trevor," Marlon called.

He straightened from the starting line. "Sir."

"Walk with us."

"Ronnie, make sure no one drowns. Cam, make sure no one cheats," Trevor called.

"Badger," they both saluted.

Trevor hopped the fence and fell into step with Marlon and Seiko as the squad took off.

"What's Oslia's main export?" Marlon asked.

"Candles, lamp oil, and soap," Seiko answered.

"All made from whales," Marlon said. "Oslia's entire economy is wrapped up in whaling. The blood dragon is targeting whaling vessels and fishing villages."

"For what purpose?"

"Blood dragons feed off terror more so than other types of dragons. Whaling ships that successfully harpoon a target are then attached to a fifty-ton carcass they must butcher as quickly as possible. The blood and blubber draws sharks for miles. The blood dragon appears to be setting the ships on fire to watch the sailors decide whether to burn to death or take their chances with the sharks."

Seiko shook his head. "That's awful."

"She raids the villages for food, but I believe she hunts the whalers for sport. If your squad can't deal with this, we will lose some very important imports."

"Understood, Raven. We'll get it done," Seiko said with a salute.

Marlon waited until Seiko was out of earshot. "Do you do that often?" he asked Trevor.

Trevor started. "Do what, sir?"

"Make Cam the standard you judge the rest of the squad by. It could breed resentment."

"Or it could push the whole squad to be better," Trevor challenged.

"He's the youngest and smallest member of your squad. There's no way he's faster than the others."

"Oh, he's not but he's not much slower than them, and he's the best swimmer we've got. He'll more than make up any ground he's lost in the water."

"Still, why single him out like this?"

"Sir, are you objecting to the way I treat my squad, or just questioning my motives?"

"He's younger even than you think he is," Marlon said softly.

Trevor's eyes widened at the implication. "I single him out, I suspect, for the same reason you allowed him to stay. He's responsible, internally motivated, and utterly incapable of underperforming. I've never once caught him out past curfew. He's an overachiever, and if I didn't push him, he'd be bored."

Marlon considered Trevor's answer before asking, "And what are you grooming him for?"

Trevor shrugged. "Something more than this. I'd say your job, if it wasn't already spoken for."

Marlon blinked in surprise and laughed. "I asked the question. I should have been prepared for the answer. Thank you, Trevor. Watch over my son while you're gone."

Trevor saluted at what was clearly a dismissal but hesitated.

"Is there something you want to ask?" Marlon said.

"Sir, do you think we're ready for this?"

Marlon sighed, looking back up at the castle. "I don't know. We've prepared you as best we can, but the only true test is the enemy and who remains standing at the end of the fight. I have faith in you, as does Kolya. If we didn't, we wouldn't send you."

"Of course. Thank you, Raven," Trevor said, saluting again.

Marlon returned his salute and watched him walk away.

*       *       *

The squad looked up when Seiko entered the room.

"Where are we going?" Nicholas asked.

"Oslia," he answered. "A blood dragon has been sighted attacking their villages."

"Scouting again?" Thomas whined.

"This is our mission," Trevor corrected.

Seiko looked around the room, meeting each of their gazes in turn. "We are to find and eliminate this monster before any more lives are lost."

"Finally!"

"A blood dragon is no easy target," Trevor cautioned. "This will test us all in ways we cannot imagine. Pack your things. We leave in the morning and we'll come home with the dragon's head or not at all."

They cheered and rushed from the room.

"You know the dragon's head is going to be too massive to even move, let alone drag all the way back to Sedria, right?" Seiko asked, lips twitching.

Trevor shrugged. "It sounded good."

*   *   *

"What can you tell us about this dragon, Shark?" Cameron asked when they were sitting around the campfire two days later.

Seiko looked around at the fire at his men. "She's a blood dragon. What does that tell you?"

"That she'll bleed just like anything else," one of them snickered, elbowing his neighboring squad member.

"Thomas," Trevor growled. Thomas stopped laughing and looked away.

"Blood dragons are always female and they feed on fear," Cameron answered, staring into the fire.

"So how does that change our tactics?" Seiko asked, poking the fire with a stick and watching it spit sparks.

"Don't be afraid," Thomas muttered sarcastically under his breath.

"Tom, if you're not going to contribute to the conversation, then shut up," Trevor snapped.

Ethan reached over and smacked Thomas on the back of the head. Thomas folded his arms across his chest, pouting, but was silent.

"Blood dragons are big and slow but are more powerful than other dragons and tend to be more animalistic in nature," Trevor said, answering the question.

Seiko looked back at the fire as the sap in the logs popped. "We're headed to Canalla, which was the last fishing village she attacked. We're going to try to determine how she chooses her targets with the hope that we can predict or even influence the location of her next strike."

"Do you really think that's possible?" Joseph asked.

"Her attacks on the villages are need-based. It's true that blood dragons feed on fear, but they also need physical sustenance. It stands to reason that if we can figure out what her specific needs are, we can predict where she'll strike next."

"Couldn't we just take a boat out to the island she's nested on and kill her in her sleep?" Aaron asked.

"Dragons don't have nests. They have dens," Cameron said. "And they're never completely asleep, right?"

"That's correct," Trevor said. "So rest up. We've got three more days of travel, and a dragon fight at the end of it."

*      *      *

They reached Canalla three days later in the late afternoon.

It had been a quiet fishing village before the blood dragon. Now, it was little more than a collection of burned, scarred buildings. The inn at the center of town seemed relatively undamaged in comparison, so that was where they headed.

As they dismounted in front of the inn, the innkeeper came out to greet them. He was a large, balding man with a scraggly beard and wisps of white hair sticking up around the crown of his head. He wore an old, stained apron that he wiped his hands on as he eyed the soldiers before him. "You're late. Dragon's already been and gone," he said, gesturing to the smoldering town.

Seiko shook his hand firmly. "We're from Sedria. Are you in charge here?"

The man shrugged. "As much as anybody is, I guess. I take it you're the dragon slayers they told us were coming, then?"

"That's correct. We were sent on behalf of the Raven of Sedria."

"Please come in. My stablehands will see to your horses."

Trevor shook his head. "The men can take care of the horses. I'm sure your people have enough to do since the attack."

The innkeeper inclined his head and led Seiko and Trevor inside.

"What can you tell us about this dragon?" Seiko asked.

"I've seen her set fire to buildings and turn young men into mummies with one breath." The innkeeper shook his head and was silent for a moment, staring out the window. Finally, he continued. "She gorges on cows, horses, and people, and burns the rest. Those of us that weren't killed might not last the year."

"We brought our own supplies. We don't intend to burden you," Trevor said.

"I appreciate that. I have no other guests at the moment. Your men can have the second floor."

"Do you mind if we ask around?" Trevor asked. "We're trying to put together a timeline."

"Not sure what else the others could tell you, but feel free," the innkeeper said and limped back into the kitchen.

Seiko turned to Trevor. "Looks like we've got our work cut out for us."

"If it were easy, someone else would have already done it," Trevor answered.

Seiko laughed.

*         *         *

Seiko entered the inn, tired after an afternoon of fruitlessly questioning villagers and sailors, many of whom had barely survived the attack. He sighed as he sat down next to Trevor. "It doesn't seem like the townspeople had any information worth sharing."

Trevor shrugged. "We knew that was a long shot. The dragon did a lot of damage. They're just trying to pick up the pieces."

"Where's Ronnie?" Seiko asked, looking around the table.

"He made a new friend," Thomas answered.

Cameron rolled his eyes. "He figured he'd be more help at the clinic. Maybe someone there saw something the others missed. Nick and Ethan are patrolling in case wolves or bandits try to take advantage of the villagers."

"I think that's as much as we can do for tonight," Trevor said with a yawn. "We should head to bed and regroup in the morning."

Seiko accepted a plate of food from Thomas. "Rotating patrols all night. I don't want anyone to say we neglected our duties."

"Shark," they said as they finished their supper quickly and went to bed.

*         *         *

Seiko woke with a start to people screaming and the smell of ash and sulfur in the air. He pulled on his boots and ran outside. "Badger, what's going on?" he called as Trevor appeared out of the smoke.

"Blood dragon's attacking!" he answered, sliding to a stop side beside him, breathing hard. "Cam and Ronnie are setting up on the far side of the village. I sent Joe and Ethan to wake the villagers and get them to safety."

Seiko coughed as he inhaled smoke. "This doesn't make sense. She's never attacked the same village twice in a row."

"Maybe we were the closest thing to her when she realized she was hungry."

The townspeople rushed around and between them, trying to flee from the fire that left nothing but ash and mummified bodies in its wake.

"No. She's a flier. Proximity is not a limiting factor. She's need-based and animalistic. There's nothing left for her here. Why attack Canalla again? What drew her back?"

"Down!" Trevor yelled, tackling Seiko as the dragon flew overhead breathing fire. "You need to focus," he snapped, leaping to his feet. "We can discuss why this is happening later."

Seiko scrambled to his feet, both of them shielding their faces with their forearms, ash and embers swirling around them. "You're right. Take me to Cam and Ronnie."

Trevor turned and began to run. "The others should be there by now."

They reached the edge of the village as the blood dragon came around again. She roared, arrows bouncing off her chest and shoulder. One managed to ricochet into her wing, and it stuck fast.

"Move!" Seiko yelled as fire rained down on them. Someone screamed, but he couldn't worry about that right now.

"She's coming back," Trevor called.

"Aim for the wings!" Seiko said. "We won't get many more shots at this."

They struck as she came around again. Two more arrows hit her wings, and a lucky shot punctured her eye. She screamed and fell, skidding across the ground. The men all dove out of the way, but Trevor was too slow. Her skid ended on the sand just outside of town. She thrashed frantically and righted herself as they ran toward her. Trevor lay beneath her, screaming.

"Trevor!" Seiko called, sliding between the dragon's legs while the others distracted her and dragged Trevor to safety.

"Shark," Trevor hissed.

Seiko looked down and realized Trevor's leg was lying at an odd angle. He cursed. "Stay here. I'll be back soon."

He grimaced and said, "Not like I have much choice," as Seiko ran back toward the dragon.

"Shark, we can't get close," Dylan shouted as he dodged the dragon's breath.

Everywhere the dragon breathed, the grass withered and died. Seiko looked down at Joseph's corpse. It was a dry withered husk, and the innkeeper's comments about mummies now made sense.

*She doesn't just feed on fear,* Seiko realized. *She feeds on life itself.*

He ran at her head as she lunged forward and grabbed Nicholas in her talons.

"Nick!" Dylan cried out.

The blood dragon rose on her hind legs, beat her wings twice, and launched herself into the air.

"No," Seiko growled as he sprinted after her.

"Shark!" Cameron called, but Seiko barely heard him.

"Seiko Kasun!" Trevor barked, his voice carrying across the field.

Seiko slid to a stop, shaking and panting, watching as the blood dragon flew out of sight. He turned and jogged back to Trevor, fists clenched. "How bad is it?"

"It's bad," Aaron answered as he tied a splint to Trevor's leg. "His leg's broken, and his knee got pretty messed up when the dragon landed on him."

Trevor hissed, head rolling back against the tree trunk.

Seiko crouched beside him. "We'll get you to a healer. They can—"

"Shark," Trevor forced through gritted teeth. "You're not thinking. There are no healers around. You're not going to be able to fix this."

"Shark!" Cameron called.

Seiko sighed and rose, walking over to where the rest of his squad was gathered, feeling an immense weight settle on his shoulders as he asked, "Who else did we lose?"

"The dragon nabbed Nick, Joe is dead, and I think Ethan's in shock," Cameron answered, motioning to where Ethan sat, arms wrapped around his knees. "The village herbalist survived the attack. The villagers are helping her organize the wounded."

Seiko looked around at their tired faces. "Ronnie, see what you can do to help triage. The rest of you, do what you can for those not in need of immediate medical attention."

"Shark," they said as he walked back to Trevor.

*        *        *

Aaron returned shortly with the herbalist. She was an older woman with silver-gray hair tied in a tight braid to keep it out of her face. She was bent with age and the hazards of her profession but her eyes were sharp. She carried a medical kit under her arm.

Aaron hefted a case with what Seiko assumed was the rest of her supplies. "This is Maple," he said, setting the case down.

Seiko cocked his head. "Maple, as in…"

"Yes, like the tree," she snapped, kneeling beside Trevor. "My mother liked the name Mabel, but naming children after plants is a tradition in my family. Anything else? Or can I examine your friend now?"

Seiko shook his head.

Maple turned to Trevor. "What's your name?"

"Trevor," he answered through gritted teeth.

She glanced over at Aaron. "You, run back to my house and get the crate of wood and pieces of cloth. We need to reset and splint this fracture."

"Yes, ma'am," he said and jogged away.

"And you," she said, looking at Seiko. "They call you Shark, right? Go get one of your men, the stronger the better. We're going to need help."

Seiko hesitated.

"You do him no good standing there. Go on and do something useful."

He bit his lip, looking at Trevor.

"Go on. I'm not going anywhere."

Seiko jogged away, calling for Thomas.

Trevor winced as Maple examined his leg. "Is it really going to take four people to set my leg?"

"Maybe more. You're guarding, and I have to reset this or it'll heal improperly and you won't ever walk again."

"That sounds like fun."

"If we do it right, you're going to try and kick someone in the head. If we do it wrong, you could die."

"Has anyone ever told you that your bedside manner leaves a lot to be desired?"

"My third husband, right before he died on me." Maple looked up as Aaron, Seiko, and Thomas returned. "Shark," she snapped. "I need you to kneel behind Trevor and hold onto him as tight as you can. Get your knees as close to him as possible. You'll want to use your legs and torso to block his movement. Trevor, cross your arms across your chest."

Seiko wrapped his arms around Trevor, who leaned against him, tense.

Satisfied, Maple turned to the other two. "Aaron, you need to be ready to splint his leg once I've got it aligned correctly."

He took a position near Trevor's knee, lengths of wood and strips of cloth in a line next to him within arm's reach, having already gone through her box of supplies.

"What's your name, boy?" she said to Thomas.

"Thomas," he replied uncertainly.

"Thomas, I need you to grab his ankle and pull as hard as you can, and hold it. You might feel something weird as the bones shift, but I need you to keep pressure until I tell you to stop. Understand?"

"Yes, ma'am," he said.

"Is everybody ready?"

"Let's get this over with," Seiko said.

"Wait, what happened to your first two husbands?" Trevor asked as Thomas gripped his leg.

"They asked too many questions," she answered. "Go."

Thomas pulled on Trevor's leg, and Trevor screamed. Seiko's grip tightened as Trevor fought to free himself. There was a sickening sound as the bones slid against each other, and Trevor went limp. Maple wrapped her hands around the fracture as it slid into place. "Aaron," she snapped, but he was already moving, wrapping the cloth and splint around the fracture.

Thomas gritted his teeth, arms shaking. "How much longer?"

She moved a wooden box under the fracture. It had half circles cut into it at either end. It was long enough that it ran from the middle of Trevor's shin to just above his knee.

"What is that for?" Seiko asked as she and Aaron tied it securely to Trevor's leg.

"Set him down gently," Maple said as they finished, ignoring the question.

Thomas obeyed then ran away, retching.

"It's to keep him from moving the leg, or anyone else from hitting it accidentally," Aaron answered.

"Is…is he dead?" Seiko asked, resting Trevor's head on a wad of leftover bandages.

"Just unconscious," Maple answered. "We'll have to move him later. Can your men construct a litter to carry him in? We may need it for other patients as well."

"We'll figure out how to make anything you need," Seiko said quietly.

"Good. The carpenter died in the first attack, but his widow should be able to help with materials." Maple rose and walked back toward the village.

"Ronnie," Seiko ordered, "go help her, and send Cam back to me if you see him."

Aaron did as he was told.

*       *       *

"Shark, what can I do to help?" Cameron asked as he approached several minutes later.

Seiko took a deep breath and forced himself to his feet. "Stay with Trevor in case he wakes up. I'll send the others back here as they finish their tasks. Aaron should be back shortly. I need the two of you to construct a litter to get Trevor back to the inn."

Cameron saluted.

Seiko turned and headed back into the village. He found the innkeeper looking even more haggard and worn, blood running from several cuts on his arms. "I need your help."

"I am trying to make sure no one starves tonight on top of everything else. What do you want?"

"I need to talk to someone who still has a boat."

"You're crazy. You want to go after that monster?"

"We came to kill it, and that hasn't changed."

"No one's crazy enough to take you out to her lair, not after what just happened."

"Please just tell me who to talk to. I lost two of my own, and I will not let it be for nothing."

The innkeeper sighed. "Talk to old man Reed. He's outlived the rest of his family and doesn't much care what happens to him. He's also the only one that's been out to the dragon's lair since she moved in."

"Thank you." He hesitated before adding, "You really should get that arm looked at."

The innkeeper snorted. "I'm still able to move. I'll deal with it when I have time, if I'm still alive."

*        *        *

Seiko walked out to the beach and saw someone working on a boat. "Are you Reed?"

The old man paused. "I am. What of it?"

"I'm looking for a boat."

"Odd time to be headed out onto the water. What do you need a boat for?"

"Same as you. To kill a dragon."

The man turned to study him. "Now why would you want to throw your life away on a fool thing like that? Your age, don't you got a girl waiting for you at home, or a mother, at least? You want to make her cry?"

"I came here to kill a dragon. She has killed two of my friends and scores of your neighbors. I will not return home while her threat remains."

The man's eyes narrowed. "Alright, boy. I'll take you out there, but I'm not doing it until morning, and I'm not staying within range. When you're done, if you're still alive, launch a firework and I'll come pick you up."

Seiko held out his hand. "That's fair. I'll see you here at sunrise."

They shook hands and Seiko headed back toward what was left of Canalla.

*     *     *

Seiko found his squad gathered around a small fire. He crouched, a mug of coffee in his hand, looking at the firelit faces of his squad, haggard and disillusioned. "I managed to convince one of the villagers to take us out to the Isle of Pation in the morning. Ethan and Ronnie," he said and waited for them to look at him. "You'll stay here and do what you can for the villagers. If we don't return in two days, you need to get back to Raven and inform him that we failed."

They both saluted. "Shark."

"Nick needs our help now!" Dylan said, fists clenched around his mug but unable to muster the motivation to stand.

"We are no use to anyone right now, as exhausted as we are. If we left now, we'd all end up dead." Seiko sighed and pushed himself to his feet. "Let's get Trevor on the litter and back to the inn."

Trevor moaned as they lifted him onto the litter, but the moans subsided once they picked it up. They carried him back to the inn and carefully laid him in one of the beds, being careful not to bump his broken leg on the doorframe.

Seiko tried to stifle a yawn. "Get some rest. We leave in the morning."

They looked at each other before filing out of the room.

Seiko grabbed a blanket and lay on the floor next to Trevor's bed, crying.

*     *     *

"Seek… Seek!" Trevor called.

Seiko looked up as the sound penetrated his mind. He had no idea how long he'd been crying, but if Trevor was awake, it must have been quite some time.

"You've got to keep it together," Trevor said.

"Shouldn't you be asleep?"

Trevor grimaced. "Yeah, I don't think that's going to happen anytime soon. Who knew a broken leg would hurt so bad?"

"I'm sorry, Trevor. It's my fault."

"What makes you say that?"

"I'm the reason she came back. She attacked because of me."

"Even if that's true, that doesn't make any of this your fault," Trevor said firmly as Seiko avoided his gaze. "Your father was good at that, wasn't he? Making you believe everything was your fault?"

Seiko took a deep breath and met Trevor's gaze. "I knew in my head that this would be brutal. I guess I just wasn't prepared for the reality."

"No one was. That's how life works sometimes." He studied Seiko for a moment. "You need to be prepared for the fact that the dragon killed Nick."

Seiko swallowed and stared at his hands, tears threatening again.

"I know, but I couldn't tell them that. I couldn't destroy their hope."

Trevor studied him for a moment. "Sleep. There's still a few hours before sunrise, and you look exhausted."

He lay back down and closed his eyes.

*               *               *

Seiko, Dylan, Thomas, Cameron, and Logan disembarked and crept quietly onto the island.

"Do you think she knows we're here?" Logan whispered.

"She knows," Cameron called as they all ducked behind boulders.

The blood dragon dove, spitting fire at them. The flames seemed to curl around the rocks, seeking living flesh.

Seiko covered his face with his arms, feeling the fire wash over him. He gritted his teeth as his skin charred and flaked off. Screams sounded around him and the air was filled with the acrid stench of burning flesh.

When the blood dragon ran out of breath, Seiko stood, arms dripping a clear silvery fluid that hissed when it hit the ground. He let out a scream of rage and launched himself into the sky as his body transformed. He was large, maybe two or three times the size of a horse, but still significantly smaller than the blood dragon. He was covered not in scales but in a shimmering, almost amphibian silver substance. He was longer and leaner with a tail that was twice the length of his body. He flew high and dove at the blood dragon.

She tucked her wings and rolled to her right.

Seiko opened his wings and barely managed to control his descent before slamming into the ground.

She turned to breathe fire on the squad but Seiko threw himself between them and the flames, screaming as the fire licked at his back. He whipped his tail at her snout, and it connected with a loud crack.

She backpedaled, glaring at him with her good eye. She breathed fire at him, and he countered with an acid spray.

The resulting explosion launched them both into the air as the island began to crack and sink.

Seiko attacked the blood dragon again, his teeth sinking into her shoulder.

She bellowed in rage and pain.

He released her and she fell, landing hard.

Dylan ran up and buried his spear in her chest, ripping it out and stepping away as fire ran from her chest.

Exhausted, Seiko's form changed and he collapsed, unconscious.

*       *       *

Seiko woke slowly, head throbbing. He was back in the inn. "Cam?" he asked, seeing him dozing in the chair next to his bed.

Cam awoke with a start at the sound of Seiko's voice, nearly falling out of his chair. "How are you feeling, Shark?" he asked as he recovered.

Seiko groaned as he sat up. "Is it dead?"

Cameron smiled. "Dylan killed it after you passed out. The archipelago sank around us, but we managed to tread water until the sailors found us. Good thing you made us all learn how to swim."

"How long?" Seiko tried to sit up but fell back against the pillows.

"Have you been out?" Cameron guessed. "Two days. Trevor sent Ethan and Dylan back to the capital once we returned to

Canalla. The others are still here helping as best they can."

Seiko watched him, eyes narrowed. "What are you not telling me?"

"Tom's been telling everyone how you turned into a dragon," Cameron said. "The fisherman almost didn't let you on the boat. I don't think we can stifle the rumors."

"I was afraid of this," Seiko said slowly, watching Cameron. "What do you think?"

He bit his lip, brow knit. "Well, we've always known you were a dragon," he said finally. "And you saved us two or three times during that fight. As far as I'm concerned, you did what you had to do."

"And if I did it again?"

Cameron looked at him. "I've seen now what those monsters are capable of. We need to do whatever is necessary to take them down."

Seiko closed his eyes and rested his head on the pillow. "How's Trevor?"

Cameron laughed. "In charge despite the leg."

"Sounds about right."

# CHAPTER 14



*He's trying to protect you.*

Seiko entered Marlon's office slowly. They hadn't spoken much in the two months since he'd returned from hunting the blood dragon. Seiko wasn't sleeping well, and his nightmares usually consisted of Joseph and Nicholas screaming.

"I've added four new members to your squad," Marlon began almost before Seiko sat down. "Jason, Troy, William, and Charles."

Seiko sat back, arms folded across his chest. "No."

"No?"

"That's right," he declared. "I will run this squad, but I will not add to the death toll."

Marlon rose and walked around his desk. "That isn't your decision to make. Your squad needs a full complement of ten."

Seiko exploded out of his chair. "You don't know what we need!"

Marlon's eyes hardened and he stared Seiko down.

"Apologies, Raven," Seiko uttered with a bow. "That was disrespectful and unwarranted."

Marlon looked at him, expression unchanged. "Apology accepted, but the situation remains unchanged."

"At least let me keep Trevor."

Marlon shook his head. "You know I can't do that. He can't fight."

"He's still a better soldier than half of these kids."

"He only has one working leg. Leaving him in your squad would get him killed."

"Leaving him with nothing will get him killed just as quickly!" Seiko shouted, blinking furiously.

"We didn't leave him with nothing. We've dealt with injured soldiers before." Marlon cocked his head. "But this isn't really about Trevor, is it? Two men under your command died, and a third will never walk unassisted again." Marlon closed the distance between them. "You feel like you failed them. Like it wouldn't have happened if you were faster, stronger, smarter. It doesn't matter what I say right now because your heart can't accept it. You didn't fail. You stumbled, and now you have two choices: you can give up, I've seen soldiers do that, or you can get up and keep going. You will make mistakes and you will lose soldiers, good men. Sometimes, it's not even going to be a mistake. You can do everything right and still lose people. It's a heavy responsibility to hold the lives of others in your hands. We all have different ways of coping." Marlon chuckled. "I find a quickly rushing river and swim against the current until I'm exhausted. Kolya usually fishes me out before I drown."

"What about Kolya?"

"We spar 'til neither of us has any strength left to pick up a weapon."

Seiko exhaled sharply. "I'll try, Raven."

"There is something else you should know," Marlon said, returning to his chair. "Aderes knows Jason as Kisko."

"What does that mean for me?"

"I'm not entirely sure. He was born within Aderes' forest, and it appears to have granted him a certain…intuition."

"He can see the future?"

Marlon shook his head. "Anyone who claims they can tell you the future with certainty is a liar. In Jason's case, he gets what he calls 'feelings,' generally about people or events as they happen, and sometimes just before."

"That doesn't sound useful or trustworthy."

"It's more useful than you might think. A five-second heads up about an ambush could save your life."

"So not only do I have to learn four new squad mates, I also have to deal with this weird mystic? I need some time."

"Your new recruits start next week. That's all the time I can afford to give you," Marlon said as he returned to his chair and began going through reports.

Seiko left, body rigid.

*       *       *

Seiko stormed across the yard and, before he knew it, found himself outside the barracks.

"Looks like your chat with Raven didn't go well," Trevor called.

Seiko looked up and saw Trevor sitting on a log. "I'm not sure why I expected any different."

"Let's go for a ride," Trevor suggested, reaching for Seiko's hand.

"Are you allowed?" Seiko asked, helping him up.

"Doc says I can go riding as long as I have an escort."

Trevor threw his arm across Seiko's shoulders, and they carefully made their way to the stables.

∗          ∗          ∗

Seiko let out a pent-up breath as the castle disappeared behind them.

"So, what happened?" Trevor asked.

"I told Argus I'd run this squad but, the truth is, I don't know if I can watch anyone else die following my orders."

"Death happens in war, Seek. You can't prevent it."

"They're just kids, and they didn't deserve to die like that!" Seiko exclaimed abruptly.

"Life isn't fair, and people rarely wait to die until you're ready. Nick and Joe died to help us kill a blood dragon. A goal which we did accomplish, so their sacrifices weren't in vain." He shrugged. "Sometimes that's all the comfort we get."

Seiko gritted his teeth, hands tightening on his reins. "I should have known she'd attack. She smelled another dragon invading her territory and reacted like any predator would."

"Stop it," Trevor growled, pulling his horse to a stop, glaring at Seiko. "You can't shoulder all the blame for a mission that was largely successful. We all made mistakes. It was the first time most of us had fought a dragon, and she caught us off guard. There are no do-overs, and we all have to live with the consequences. We made the best decisions we could with the information available to us at the time. You make the best of it and move on. You don't quit just because you don't like the way things turned out."

"They're dead," Seiko shot back. "And I see their faces every time I close my eyes."

"I know," Trevor said soothingly. "But you can't allow every soldier's death to affect you personally. They know they may be called on to give their lives on any given mission, and they trust you to act wisely and not waste that sacrifice. There will be deaths, and sometimes you will have to choose who lives and, by extension, who dies. That is the burden of command, and you have to find a way to live with that."

Seiko realized he had a white-knuckle grip on his reins. He closed his eyes, forcing himself to relax. "What will you do now?"

"Raven has asked me to be a special weapons consultant."

Seiko opened his eyes and looked at him. "What does that entail?"

"Right now, it means improving our weapons, defenses, and tactics for fighting a dragon."

"And how are you supposed to do that?"

"I have a few ideas. Between my father training me to be a blacksmith and my mother's tutelage as an apothecary, it's a pretty good fit. I'll start with finding a way to more reliably ground a dragon."

"That sounds like something you'll need to test."

"Raven has offered a standing bounty for dragon parts, and he's given me access to one of the wings from that first dragon you killed."

They rode back to the castle lost in thought.

*      *      *

Seiko crept out of the house that night and strolled the castle wall, checking on the soldiers. He left his signet ring on the wall for Jocelynn to find. He knew how busy she was and rarely called her to Traitor's Grove, but after everything that happened, he needed to see her. He needed to talk to the Black Falcon.

He looked up as the branch he was sitting on began to sway.

"Hey," Jocelynn said and sat down beside him.

"Hey," he said, looking down at his hands.

"I heard what happened."

"Are you going to insist that it wasn't my fault too?"

Jocelynn took his hand. "I've never experienced losing someone under my command. I theoretically understand what you're going through, but I have no idea what it actually feels like. All I can say is that I'm here for you."

He squeezed her hand. "Thanks, Joy. That means more than you know."

She leaned her head against his shoulder as he began to cry.

They sat there for a long time.

*      *      *

"Who would you suggest as your replacement?" Seiko asked as he helped Trevor install railings around the smithy.

"Honestly? Cam."

"Cam?" Seiko repeated.

"You disagree?"

"I guess I'm not sure. That's not what I expected."

"Who did you think I was going to suggest?"

"I'm not sure, it's just that Cam's the youngest member of the squad."

"Cam is very young," Trevor agreed. "But age can be overcome provided he has the mind for it, and he's as experienced as any of the others."

Seiko cocked his head.

"He's eager to learn and picks things up quickly. He didn't even know what chess was before I taught him how to play. Now he beats me regularly. He respects ability and has a history of dealing with people who are older than him. Half of the squad already defers to him whether or not they'll admit it," Trevor explained.

"It's a lot to ask of a man who saw two of his friends die and one of his commanding officers maimed."

"It will be a challenge, but I wouldn't have suggested him if I didn't think he could handle it. I would also recommend that Raven promote Cam, Ronnie, and Ethan but make sure that Cam outranks the others. And I would let Thomas leave."

"Marlon's already replaced him."

"Good," Trevor said. "I asked him to."

"Why would you do that?"

"Because this isn't what he signed up for, Seek. He's terrified of you and no longer an asset to this squad."

Seiko ran a hand through his hair. "You're sure about Cam?"

Trevor laughed. "I'm not sure about anything. Do you think there's a better option?"

"No," he finally admitted. "Ronnie's a medic, and Ethan is still too eager to please his peers. Logan and Dylan are good at their jobs, but the kind of strategy and tactics needed for this goes over both of their heads."

"See, you know your men better than you think you do," Trevor said, smiling.

Seiko laughed as they headed back to the castle.

*                *                *

Months later, Tarik and Seiko were in the courtyard getting ready for a ride when a stablehand led Jocelynn's horse out. Seiko looked up and smiled brightly as Jocelynn entered the courtyard.

"Ready?" she asked.

"When you are," he answered.

Tarik looked at Seiko. "Did you invite her?"

Seiko shrugged. "She likes to come riding with us. Has that

suddenly become a problem?"

Tarik turned away, body rigid. "She's too old to be hanging out with us."

Seiko forced a laugh and mounted, hoping Tarik would drop the issue.

Jocelynn mounted, and the three of them rode out the gate.

"I haven't seen you in a while. What have you been up to?" Seiko asked.

Jocelynn rolled her eyes. "Mother has me in etiquette classes and dancing lessons."

"That's not so bad. Those are things you're going to need to know."

"She'd be better off teaching me how to not fall asleep in boring conversations," she said.

"Ladies' conversations are about embroidery and poetry. They're all boring," Tarik interjected from behind them.

Jocelynn stuck her tongue out at him. "We also talk about boys."

Tarik rolled his eyes.

"At least that's interesting," Seiko said with a grin.

"Not hardly. All they want to talk about are the two of you."

"Oh? And what are the girls saying about me?"

"Like I would tell you. Your head's big enough already."

Seiko laughed but he could feel Tarik glaring at him as they rode back to the castle.

*       *       *

Seiko was up in the castle arcade when Tarik found him that night. "This has to stop," Tarik told him.

"What, my insomnia?" Seiko asked lightly. "That'd be nice."

"You know what I mean."

Seiko glared at him. "I'm not sure I do. Maybe you should explain it to me."

"My sister is sixteen years old," Tarik ground out. "She should be wearing dresses, learning princess things, and cultivating friendships with girls of her age of similar status. You can't keep encouraging her to wear my pants and do guy stuff with us every chance she gets."

"I'm not encouraging anything."

Tarik folded his arms across his chest.

"What do you want me to do?" Seiko asked in exasperation.

"Stop talking to her."

Seiko laughed. "So I'm just supposed to ignore the princess of the castle I live in if she talks to me?"

Tarik rolled his eyes. "Then stop inviting her to go on rides and stuff with us."

"Is this about her being the princess, or about you feeling left out?" Seiko challenged.

"This is about her acting like a princess," Tarik snapped. "You're right. You can't just ignore her, but you shouldn't be actively seeking her out and distracting her."

Seiko backed down, realizing he'd pushed too far. "Fine. No more extracurriculars with the princess."

Tarik sniffed and watched him. Seiko held his breath, wondering how far Tarik was willing to take this argument. Eventually, he just turned and walked away, muttering something about annoying girls.

Seiko shook his head and went to find Jocelynn out on patrol in the castle as the Black Falcon.

"What's going on?" she hissed as he pulled her into a dark alcove.

"Meet me in Traitor's Grove in two hours," Seiko said.

"Alright," she said, and he released her, fading into the darkness.

*　　　　　　*　　　　　　*

Two hours later, Jocelynn climbed into their tree in Traitor's Grove. Seiko was already waiting for her.

"What's wrong?" she asked him.

"I'm leaving."

"You're leaving?" she repeated, breath caught in her throat. "What does that mean? Where are you going?"

He smiled. "Easy, there. Argus is sending me to Ferr Kenar."

"The island school for warriors?"

"Yes. Argus won't tell me the exact date, but I suspect it'll be sometime in the next two weeks."

"How long will you be gone?"

"Ferr Kenar doesn't work like that, or so I've been told. You stay until you're ready to leave."

"And you're going by yourself?" She bit her lip.

"Yes. Why does that worry you so much?"

"It's just… Marlon graduated from Ferr Kenar. As far as I know, he's the only one they have ever graduated as both Wolf and Raven. With that and the fact that you're a dragon… It puts a target on you."

Seiko paused, considering his response. Her fears mirrored his. "Argus still refuses to talk about his time on the island. Some of that is school policy but…something happened on that island. Something I think only Kolya knows about," he said softly. "But to be named both Wolf and Raven…" He shook his head. "The physical strength and mental acuity required for that is intimidating. I am not Argus, and I thank the Watchers that he's never asked me to be. But you are correct, the expectations will be high. I have yet to fail a trial Argus has set before me, and I don't intend to let him down now. I will learn everything Ferr Kenar has to teach, and then I will return, and it will be your turn."

"You really think they'll send me?" she asked.

"In time. You will be the Wolf of Sedria. That means that you must be the best of the best, and that is what this school turns young men and women into."

"Will you tell me about it when you get back?"

He laughed. "I will tell you what I can, but Ferr Kenar prides itself on secrecy, and everyone's experience is different."

"So why else did you call me out here in the middle of the night?" she asked, playfully bumping his shoulder.

He cocked his head. "What does that mean?"

"Just that we knew at some point your father would send you to Ferr Kenar, so that revelation did not necessitate an emergency clandestine meeting in Traitor's Grove. What else is going on?"

"Tarik has decided that it's time for you to act like a princess," he said, rolling his eyes.

"Well, we knew it had to happen eventually. He was only going to tolerate my presence for so long. What did he say?"

"He tried to get me to stop talking to you altogether," he answered with a laugh. "I convinced him that was stupid, but he still doesn't want you hanging out with us anymore, and he'll probably say something if he catches us talking too often."

She twisted the ring on her finger. "He'll grow out of it, right?"

"I doubt it. I think he's trying to protect you."

"From what?"

"From me," Seiko said softly. Jocelynn looked at him in confusion. "Our relationship, yours and mine, is unconventional. No one's going to believe that I'm not trying to take advantage of you."

"But you're not," she protested. "And I don't care what anyone else thinks."

He smiled sadly as she took his hand in both of hers and rested her head against his shoulder. "You will. It's easier to stay unnoticed if you adhere to expectations, and as the Black Falcon, you need to remain unnoticed."

Her eyes widened. "What if I need to get a message to you?"

"Well, there's no rule that says I can't talk to the Black Falcon, just the princess. I've already started working on a written code to help us communicate, but I'm going to need your help."

She smiled up at him. "Meet me here tomorrow night?"

"Deal."

The two of them spent the rest of the week developing a rudimentary written code consisting mainly of verbs and places. The tone was conveyed in the way the note was folded. They would use this code for the rest of their lives.

# Glossary of Mekan Words and Phrases

**Akyrier:** Star warrior or dragon.

**Kisko:** Son of fate/fated son.

**Na'ain threla:** Call of the void.

**Ser na'gire disa na'zdis zaler gire:** Our existence doesn't make us monsters, our choices do.

**Tukiko:** Son of the moon.

**Zakyri:** Stars/celestial powers.

**Zoren:** Terrestrial elementals.

# About the Author

Micah Johnson writes fantasy/speculative fiction that explores growth and maturity. Every story is a learning experience and discovery for both the characters and the reader. She lives in Florida with her amazingly patient border collie, Phantom.

www.ingramcontent.com/pod-product-compliance
Lightning Source LLC
Chambersburg PA
CBHW030901200726
48289CB00003B/850